My Dearest Emerson

Cowboy Crossing
Book 6

Jessie Gussman

Contents

Acknowledgments

Cover art by Julia Gussman
Editing by Heather Hayden
Narration by Jay Dyess
Author Services by CE Author Assistant

———

Listen to the unabridged audio for FREE performed by Jay Dyess on the Say with Jay channel on YouTube. Get early access to all of Jay's recordings and listen to Jessie's books before they're available to the general public, plus get daily Bible readings by Jay and bonus scenes by becoming a Say with Jay channel member.

To Alexa Verde.
Without you, there would be no Cowboy Crossing. Thank you for your friendship and advice. You've held my hand through some of the rockiest parts of being an author, and I could see Jesus through you.

Chapter One

This airline fuel shortage thing could end up being a real problem.

Reid Hudson waited at the St. Louis International Airport for his son, Houston, to come around the corner and down the hall.

Houston had been flying most of his life, and even the long trip from Switzerland to St. Louis didn't faze him.

In fact, both of his twin boys were perfectly okay with long flights.

They had to be, since he and his estranged wife, Emerson, had been flying them back and forth between Switzerland and St. Louis, Missouri, for most of their lives.

Dallas, Houston's twin brother, fidgeted beside Reid.

Dallas took after Reid. Impulsive. Headstrong. And a lot more likely to open his mouth and say a bunch of things he shouldn't.

Possibly, those were all characteristics that had led to the fact that he lived in Cowboy Crossing, Missouri, and his high school sweetheart, whom he married the summer after they graduated from college, now lived in Switzerland.

Normally, Dallas would be on an airplane heading toward Switzerland as he waited to pick Houston up.

But the fuel shortage had messed up all the flights, not just in St. Louis, but all over the country, and internationally as well.

Because, of course, Reid had waited until the last minute and hadn't been able to book a flight for Dallas until three days from now. It had never been a problem before.

Emerson had not been happy.

She'd insisted that she get to spend three extra days with the boys in Switzerland the next time they switched.

Dallas bounced on his toes as people started coming down the hall. As the passageway filled, he jumped higher and higher to make himself taller to try to see over their heads. He wanted to be the first to see his brother.

Deliberately, Emerson and Reid did not let the boys spend a lot of time together. They had decided early on that was best for everyone, since it was hard for the boys, once they had spent a bunch of time playing together, to leave each other.

Maybe it seemed heartless, but they'd been able to keep their arrangement now for almost a decade. Eight years and three months, if one was counting, which Reid assured himself that he was not.

"Careful, son. It's getting crowded, and you don't want to hit anyone."

He understood Dallas's excitement. He also understood his inability to be still. That had been him his whole childhood.

Out of all of his brothers, he had been the one that had been in trouble the most for not being able to sit still in church. For not being able to keep his mouth shut. For talking back or just plain talking.

How many times had he been sent to the principal's office for whispering to his neighbor in school? A couple of times he'd even gotten in trouble because his teacher had thought he was cheating.

He'd never cheated—dishonesty wasn't one of his many flaws—and thankfully his parents had believed him, although he had been disciplined for the talking.

Constant talking, constant motion, impulsive and reckless.

Yep. Dallas had it all.

"This is his plane, isn't it, Dad?" Dallas had quit jumping like he'd asked him to, but he still leaned up on his tiptoes, trying to keep his balance by swinging his arm.

A grumpy-looking, balding businessman shot an irritated glance at Dallas as he ducked the flying hand, his large black suitcase twisting and rolling behind him as he moved out of the way.

Dallas didn't even notice.

The man gave Reid a glance that communicated clearly the man's opinion of a father who couldn't control his child.

"Sorry about that, sir." Reid put a hand on Dallas's shoulder. "Be careful, son. Watch the people around you. You can't get so caught up in yourself that you don't notice where your body is in space and whether or not your appendages are flying dangerously close to other people."

Dallas looked at him with a quizzical expression. "What'd I do, Dad?"

Yeah, that's exactly what he thought. Dallas didn't even know. "Just try to stand still so you don't hit anybody."

Once again, Reid wondered at his mom's amazing ability to be patient and firm. He didn't recall her ever losing her temper at him, even though he knew he'd been exactly like Dallas. How had she done it with five other boys?

"I'm just trying to see Houston, Dad. Do you think something happened to him? Why isn't he first?"

The question made Reid smile. Dallas was always first off the airplane. Just like Reid would be if he were travelling.

He supposed when Dallas got older they'd probably butt heads because they were so much alike, but for now, Reid knew when he went to pick up Dallas, it would be an in and out, fast and furious kind of deal.

Whereas with Houston, he was much more likely to wait until the very end...

Yeah. He could see Houston now, walking along beside an elderly gentleman who had a cane in one hand and was waving a pointer finger with the other. Houston was looking at the older man and nodding solemnly.

That was Houston. A good audience for anyone. And just as slow as his brother was fast.

Very similar to how Emerson had been with Reid. Total opposites.

But they fit. Perfectly. And complemented each other with his weaknesses being her strengths, and vice versa.

When they'd first started dating, there had been several people who had said they were so opposite they probably wouldn't get along, but that had not been true.

Their separation had nothing to do with their opposite personalities.

It had everything to do with Reid's stubbornness.

And everything to do with Emerson's aversion to risk.

Money played a part too.

"Houston!" Dallas yelled. So loud even jaded travelers lifted weary heads to see what the commotion was.

Dallas didn't pay any attention, probably didn't notice, but took off running for his brother. Emerson and he had been so successful at keeping them apart that it had been about four years since they'd seen each other.

That year they'd spent Christmas with Emerson and New Year's with Reid. Emerson and he had agreed the separation for the twins after seeing each other had been too hard. And neither one of them wanted to go six months without seeing one of their children.

The discussion had been quite unemotional.

There hadn't been a divorce, and they didn't seem to have a problem being civil in their emails.

When Dallas got to where Houston was, he wrapped his arms around his brother, dragging him in a circle, with Houston letting go of his luggage and being careful not to bump the elderly man beside him. All the other passengers had gone on ahead, and he and that man were the last ones left.

Reid strode ahead, not technically supposed to be going that way, but figuring the twenty-five feet he was going to be walking wouldn't get him into much trouble.

The boys were talking a mile a minute—Dallas was talking a mile a minute and Houston was listening with a huge grin on his face—so Reid stuck out his hand to the elderly gentleman, who looked up at him underneath heavy white brows, his brown eyes sharp and perceptive.

"I'm Reid Hudson, and that was my son, Houston."

The man's gnarled hand gripped his with a surprising strength. "He's quite a young fellow. A seasoned traveler, so I hear. And a good listener." The older man's lips parted in a self-depreciating smile. "He listened to me run on about life on the farm when I was a kid growing up. He said you guys had a place in the southern part of the state." The man looked at him expectantly.

"Yeah. We do." Reid wasn't sure how much longer he was going to be farming. He'd made a couple of really bad decisions, and he was on the verge of losing everything. Not even his family knew. He would have to tell them eventually, probably by the new year.

"Well, it's probably a lot different than it was when I was a kid. We didn't have electricity, we had to get water from the well, and we used horses, because we were too poor to afford a tractor."

Reid nodded. It was different all right. Maybe not better.

"Your kid said you just put in a big new dairy barn, with all electronic equipment. But then something happened, and you don't even have cows now."

Reid just nodded, although the man was peering at him like he wanted an explanation. Reid didn't have one other than he took a risk, lost a milk contract he thought he had in the bag, and was left holding a banknote to the tune of way more than he could pay.

Not something he wanted to hash out in the airport with a stranger.

"Dad!" a female voice from behind him called, and the older gentleman's face wreathed into a smile, wrinkling up like the folds of an accordion.

"Excuse me," he said, and he shuffled off.

Reid didn't turn around to watch him leave. Instead, he took three steps to his boys and wrapped his arms around both of them, picking them up and squishing them in a group hug.

They were probably too old for it, and they would soon be too big for him to pick up anyway. He wanted to take advantage of these last few years while he was still bigger than they were.

They weren't too old to enjoy it, and their skinny little boy arms came out and wrapped around his neck and back.

"Missed ya, son. You've been off drinking hot chocolate and skiing in the Alps, letting your old man do all the farmwork by himself."

"Hey, Dad. You had me," Dallas protested.

"And that's another thing, you left me with this crazy kid that acts just like me. Can't sit still, can't stop talking, and has about six thousand ideas every three seconds."

"That's because he takes after you. That's what Mom says anyway," Houston said seriously.

Reid set the boys down and grinned. "Your mom and I don't agree on everything, but I suppose that's something she's right about. As much as it pains me to say it." He was kinda teasing about that. He never said anything bad about Emerson to the boys. Nothing more than he would tease her about if she were with them.

That had been one of their unspoken rules.

They got along so well that once in a while, okay, about once a day, Reid wondered if he ought to get on a plane and fly to Switzerland. He'd regretted their split since the day she left. And he never stopped loving her.

But he supposed a man had his pride. A lot of times it was a stumbling block.

"I can't believe we get three whole days together," Dallas said, bouncing around Houston. "I have everything all planned out. If it's warm enough, we're going to go camping, and we're going to go swimming, too. And we can spend some time with the cousins, but not too much, because we need to spend time together since we never see each other. And they're in school anyway. And Dad said we don't have to do school for the three days that we're here. We'll have to make it up some other time. But don't tell Mom until it's over, or she won't let us. Because she'll be upset, because she's real strict about school. You know. And Dad said that Uncle Loyal might let us borrow some of his horses, and we can take a trail ride. We can stay at Grandma's house one night, but no more, because we have to go camping too. We only have three days." Dallas wasn't nearly done, but Reid interrupted him.

"Come on, boys, let's head out to the truck. Is that all the luggage you have?" Reid asked, looking at the suitcase Houston had sitting beside him.

"Yeah. I've pretty much outgrown everything, and Mom said you're gonna have to buy me new clothes while I'm here. She didn't bother sending any of the stuff that was too small."

Dallas put his arm around him, and Houston returned the gesture.

"You have no idea how angry Mom was when she found out you weren't going to be there when you were supposed to be." He shook his head and looked up at Reid. "I think if you'd been there, she would've yelled at you. Although I've never actually heard Mom yell. But I'm pretty sure she would've. Because her face was really red."

Reid's lips twitched. He tried not to let them turn up.

He put an arm around Dallas and an arm around Houston and turned them toward the exit. "I guess it's a good thing I'm half the globe away from her. I wouldn't want to get yelled at."

He could tell the boys that Emerson had yelled at him once before.

It wasn't a good memory. Although at the time, in the heat of the moment, even though he was more angry at her than he'd ever been at anybody in his entire life, he remembered very clearly thinking how beautiful she was.

It wasn't that she was a raving beauty. Everyone else in school had considered her very average, he supposed. She had those flashing brown eyes and that dark hair that reminded him of an expensive walnut floor. Shiny and swirled and so alive.

Even when he was angry at her, he couldn't keep from admiring her.

Unfortunately, it hadn't been enough to keep them together.

He'd been twenty-four and young and dumb. Now, at thirty-two, he wished he'd just swallowed his pride and done what she wanted him to.

Even though he was between them, his boys—Dallas—still chattered, making plans, telling stories. Guilt pushed hard in his chest. The best memories of his childhood were of playing with his brothers. And yet, because of his stubbornness, not only had he lost his wife, but his boys had lost the opportunity to get to know each other. And of course, there were no siblings.

He wasn't the slightest bit interested in remarrying. Emerson had been all he'd ever wanted.

He could only hope she felt the same, since she'd never asked for a divorce.

When the boys came back from staying with her, sometimes he'd gently probe to see if there was a boyfriend. He never heard of any. He kind of hoped she felt the same way he did, even if they never spent another day together.

Chapter Two

Emerson Mahoney Hudson paced in her large, airy office. The Swiss Alps dominated the landscape outside her window. Snow-covered, soaring, and majestic, they never failed to inspire her as she stood in front of her window.

She stopped in front of said window and looked out, her arms crossed over her chest.

"I need to get those reports out to our processing team. If we're going to move on that new factory, we need to get this rolling. We've been stalling long enough while the environmentalists brought their lawsuits about the groundwater and the spotted sparrow." Sherman Townsend, her father's right-hand man and second-in-command only to her, had his butt on her desk, his feet crossed at the ankles, and, if she knew Sherman, his arms crossed over his chest too. She didn't turn from the window to check if she was right.

Her dad would like nothing more than to see them together, but that was never going to happen.

"Of course, Sherman. I'm almost through them. And they look good." She continued to study the picturesque view. One she would never grow tired of. Her voice was level and full of confidence, the way she wanted it to be.

Nothing of her struggle, nothing of the kerfuffle with her children showed in her tone or posture. She'd been doing this for a little over eight years. Eight years and three months to be exact, but she certainly wasn't counting. Unless she was counting the time that she got to enjoy the view and living in this wonderful country.

You prefer the little hometown you grew up in. That crazy voice in her head would never be quiet. Never be satisfied.

It was right. But she shushed it. Every day, she looked at her view and told herself she loved it more than anything, that she was grateful to live here, that she loved her job, and that she was happy alone.

All lies.

The only thing she was happy about was being able to work at a job where she could have her son with her constantly. Whichever one happened to be spending his six months with her.

She loved them both, but it had been getting harder and harder when Dallas was with her.

He was the spitting image of his father, and he reminded her of all the reasons she'd fallen in love with Reid.

Of all the reasons why she loved him still.

Of all the reasons why Sherman would never be more than a shadow sitting behind her.

Or any man. No man could be to her what Reid had been. What Reid was.

Of course, it was Reid's fault she didn't have Dallas with her now, since he'd neglected to make the arrangements for the airfare, and with the fuel shortage, flights had been limited.

She'd been so looking forward to seeing Dallas again. If only because seeing Dallas was like seeing Reid, and she'd been unreasonably upset that she was going to have to wait longer than she expected. Even while she had to smile at the fact that *of course* Reid waited until the last minute to make airfare arrangements. She should have done it herself. He was always busy on the farm with harvest this time of year.

"Emerson?"

Sherman's voice cut into her thoughts. She closed her eyes with frustration. She'd been doing a very good job hiding the turmoil in her chest, hadn't she?

Drat the stupid man's pride anyway. She'd thought Reid would come for her. She never imagined for one second he'd let her leave and not even make an attempt to come get her and bring her back.

Maybe there was a little bit of pride involved for her too. Since she wasn't going home unless he came for her.

She turned, her arms falling down to her sides as she strode back over to the desk and stood in front of the laptop, punching a few buttons.

"Yes?" she said in her haughtiest voice to Sherman. Haughty, because she had no idea what he'd just said to her. And haughty also because she didn't want him in her office hanging out.

She'd always been very clear about where she stood on personal issues—completely closed off to them.

At just the slightest sign from her, Sherman would be making a move—he'd been clear about that. She didn't want to make things awkward, but she wasn't interested. And she couldn't let him forget that, not for one second.

"Your dad specifically told me that we were to work together on this. I'm willing to go over those reports with you. If they need to be turned in tomorrow, I can make it a late night."

Sherman had straightened when she'd walked over, and he towered over her. With his blond hair and athletic, skiing physique, he was every inch the handsome Swiss. Although he respected her and his tone was all business.

She'd turned him down multiple times for ski trips, coffee, and when he flat-out asked her on a date two years ago. All noes.

He'd quit asking, and she occasionally saw or heard about him out with someone. Not her.

"I know what Dad said. And we are. We're just not looking at the reports together. We're still doing the project together. I think that's what he meant. Thanks for your help. Have a good evening."

She looked up with a tight smile and clear disinterest before looking back down and typing some more on her laptop. Pulling up her email, she checked to see if Reid had sent his typical message that Houston had arrived safely.

His name was there in bold print, and her heart skipped a beat.

Sherman strode to the door, walking out, and she barely noticed.

Reid Hudson. His name. How many times in high school had she scribbled it on her notebook? His name with her name. Then they were a couple, and she kept scribbling his name and her name together. Reid. Hudson.

She opened the email and read his terse words.

Houston arrived safely.
Reid.

That was it. She never wrote anything more than that, either, when it was her turn.

Still, seeing his name in her inbox gave her a thrill.

Despite that, she supposed it was time for her to get over him. She didn't want to get to the end of her life and realize she spent it pining over a man who was so stubborn he would rather hold onto his pride than love her.

———

Houston Hudson lay on the creek bank, his legs dangling over the edge and his bare feet submerged in the water. His hands were clasped behind his head, and he looked at the sky which had turned a golden blue.

He'd been thinking about something pretty hard the last two

days, and he thought it was about time that he brought his brother into his confidence.

Dallas splashed through the creek, bending over and lifting rocks, trying to find crayfish, but then he'd get distracted by the minnows which were swimming by and try to catch those.

Houston's pants were soaked, not because he'd been in the creek, but because his brother had been splashing all around him, getting him wet.

He didn't mind. He definitely liked having his brother around. It made things interesting and exciting. Dallas thought of things he never would. Like taking the matches out to the driveway and playing with them. Their dad had been fine with it, as long as they didn't set themselves on fire.

Houston wasn't sure he'd ever met anybody who'd actually set themselves on fire on purpose. But they dutifully promised not to, and his dad shrugged on his way out to the barn.

Normally he and Dallas, when they were with him by themselves, trotted after their dad wherever he went.

But since they only had three days to play together, their dad let them off almost all their normal chores and allowed them pretty much free rein.

Dallas had also come up with the idea of swinging on the grapevine in the woods.

Thankfully, when it snapped, Houston hadn't broken any bones when he fell to the ground.

It hurt for a little bit, and he'd had trouble catching his breath, but the fun they'd had up until it broke was totally worth it.

Dallas had also had the really great idea of digging themselves a cave. Of course, Houston had to do most of the work, because Dallas had gotten bored after about ten minutes. It wasn't completely done, but Houston planned to work on it if his other plans didn't work out.

Thinking of that, he propped himself up on his elbows and waited for Dallas to stop splashing so he could hear him.

"Dallas?" he said.

Dallas's head popped up, and the face that looked so much like Houston's own looked right back at him. "What?" Dallas looked around, even though Houston hadn't made any motions like he was trying to get him to see something.

"I want to talk to you about something." He narrowed his eyes at his brother. "Something important. Something we can't tell Dad about."

Suspicion, combined with eagerness, entered his brother's eyes. Houston could almost see them warring with each other. Yeah, Dallas was a bundle of energy and never stopped. He had great ideas, and he was pretty spontaneous. But he wasn't a bad kid. He was honest and forthright.

The kind of kid that Houston would want to be friends with.

The kind of kid that Houston *did* want to be friends with. That was the whole point of this plan.

"If Dad asks me, I can't lie to him." Dallas kicked the water, and Houston didn't even flinch when the spray landed over his upper legs. "Oh boy, I'm sorry. I knew it was gonna splash, just didn't know the water was gonna go there."

"It's okay. We're in the creek. We're supposed to get wet."

He really didn't mind. Maybe he'd rather not be wet, but he'd rather have a brother to play with and be wet than to be completely dry and be by himself.

"I don't expect you to lie to Dad. But I don't think he's going to ask us about this."

"I can't lie to Mom either."

"I'm not asking you to lie. I don't believe in lying either. I hate liars." He almost spit, but he wasn't entirely sure of how his brother felt about spitting. And he didn't want to do anything that was going to upset him. Not that Dallas seemed like the kind of kid that cared. They'd probably have spitting contests if his plan worked out.

"Then what is it? Come on. You have an idea? We can do your idea. Tell me." Dallas came over and sat on the bank beside Houston, swinging his legs and making his bare feet drag in the water.

Houston pushed himself up, knowing that Dallas wouldn't be able to sit still. "I want to be with you all the time. I don't like having a brother but not having a brother. Do you know what I mean?"

"Yep," Dallas said. "It sucks to never get to play with you. You're the best person to play with ever."

They weren't supposed to say that word, but Houston didn't remind him of that. Not now.

"I think I figured out a way that we might be able to get to spend more time together." He bit his lip, unsure if he'd be able to get Dallas to pay attention long enough to get through the whole plan.

But he needn't have worried. Dallas even stopped swinging his legs. He leaned a little closer. "Really? How?"

Houston usually took a while to get his thoughts together and form his words. He didn't like to have to rush. But he needed to say things quickly, or Dallas might lose interest.

"Well, first of all, what we need to do is to get Mom and Dad together."

"That's never gonna happen. They live in different countries." Dallas said that like that was common knowledge and common sense.

Which it was. Except... "Dad's pretty relaxed, but Mom gets upset. Not easily, but when she does, she moves to fix things. We need to do something so Mom feels like she needs to move to fix it." Houston looked at Dallas, hoping Dallas would kind of understand what he was trying to say.

But no light dawned in Dallas's eyes. He bit his fingernail, turning his head and spitting.

Yeah. That's what Houston thought. Dallas didn't mind spitting. Another time.

For now... "I have a plan. Two plans actually. You ready?"

"Sure. Shoot," Dallas said, but his feet were swinging again, so Houston knew he needed to hurry.

"You need to miss your flight. I mean, you need to get on the flight, because Dad has to watch until you're on, and then Dad needs to leave, and I'll make sure he goes quickly, then you need to get back off it." Houston had been thinking about it. Because of the fuel shortage and the lack of flights, every flight was jampacked, the airports were crowded and crazy. There was also a big long list of people waiting to see if a seat opened up.

Generally, it had been confusion at the airports. More so than usual.

Dallas was bouncing back and forth on his butt, but the expression on his face was thoughtful. In Houston's experience, with the little bit of time that he got to spend with his brother, Dallas thought better if he was moving.

Unfortunately, Houston thought better if he was sitting still.

But since he'd already been thinking about this, and Dallas needed to get things straightened out in his brain. Houston pushed up, threw his body out, and landed in the creek.

"Come on. Let's look for crawfish while you think about it."

Dallas didn't need a second invitation. He was jumping off before Houston even finished talking. Splashing through the creek, he went over to the other side where the bigger rocks were.

"Help me with this one. It's too heavy for me."

That was probably too heavy for crawfish to be under, but Houston didn't say that. He just went over and stuck his hands next to Dallas's. "Pull on three, okay?"

"Sure," Dallas said. "One, two, three." They groaned and strained, and finally the rock popped out.

To Houston's surprise, there were three crayfish underneath it.

How could that be? The rock was so heavy they could barely lift it, and yet there were three crayfish under there.

He had to be quick, grabbing them right behind the front pinchers.

"I'll get this one." He pointed to the biggest one.

"I'll get the other two. Both hands," Dallas said, his word sounding snippy almost, but it was because he was excited. He scrunched down, both hands raised over the crawfish. "I think I can do it. And you think that'll bring Mom?"

"I don't know." That was the iffy part of his plan. His mom didn't like to travel. She did it for the company, but she was adamant about never going back to Missouri. He'd asked. Pretty much every time he went to Switzerland. It was nice and all, but if he could choose, Missouri was where he wanted to be. With his mom *and* his dad.

It's where his grandparents were.

His other grandfather, Mom's dad, was in Switzerland. But he wasn't any fun.

Dallas's hands shot out, each one snatching a crayfish.

Houston bit his lip and thought about the angle that his hand would have to come down to hit the back right behind the pinchers.

"Even if she doesn't come, it's going to take a while before Dad can get another flight. I heard Mom talking before I left, and it's possible that all the airlines will shut down, and nobody will be getting any flights. Maybe, if you miss one, there won't be another one."

Houston could see Dallas liked that idea. He smiled and bit his tongue. Then his hand shot out, and he snatched up the last crayfish. "Yes! Got him."

"Actually..." Dallas squinted at the crustacean. "It's smaller than I thought it was. I think it's a girl."

Houston wasn't sure that size had anything to do with it being male or female, but he didn't want to get sidetracked into a discussion about crayfish just yet.

Dallas held both crayfish at chest level while his eyes sought Houston's. "Do you really think it's that bad? You don't think I'll be able to get another flight? You think we'll get to stay here, like, a long time?"

"Maybe we can figure out another plan to get Mom to come, if this doesn't do it."

"But we don't need Mom. If there aren't any flights, she can't come anyway. But if you and I are together, it doesn't matter if Mom's here."

Houston didn't want to wait for Dallas to put everything

together. He would, eventually. But he needed to take the time to think about it. And Houston didn't have that kind of time. They needed to make plans.

"If Mom comes, maybe she and Dad will decide that they still like each other, and she'll stay." He stared at Dallas, trying to get Dallas to understand the importance of what he had just said.

For once, Dallas went totally still. They stared at each other, their mouths open. Then Dallas's mouth curved slowly into a smile. It mirrored Houston's.

Houston wrinkled his nose and nodded, and Dallas imitated him.

"I gotcha. Mom and Dad...need to fall in love."

Chapter Three

Reid hated this part.

He stood in front of the long line of chairs at the airport terminal, his arms wrapped around Dallas, fighting back tears. He hated watching his boy walk away. Either one of them.

Usually it was a little easier to see Dallas go, because a quick hug was all he wanted before he was moving on to the next thing. Typically, Reid was just praying he'd be able to stay seated in his seat and not try to jump out of the plane before it landed.

He hoped his kid was smart enough to at least know he needed a parachute, but sometimes Dallas was just like him, and his brain didn't always make sense.

Reid could relate.

But for some reason today, Dallas seemed to be clinging. Unusual. Maybe it was the preteen hormones.

Reid didn't really remember feeling any effects like this in him at that time. And Dallas seemed to be a clone. Still. They were bound to be different in some areas.

Of course, maybe it was because he'd gotten to spend three days with his brother. That had always been a problem.

The special boarding pass he had for children allowed him to come back with his son, and because Houston was only ten, he was allowed to come along. Dallas let go of Reid and immediately grabbed his brother in a bear hug. That pierced Reid's soul.

Dallas seemed really torn up about leaving, which was, again, very uncharacteristic. In fact, was that a tear?

"I'm so glad we got to spend time together. I'll never forget you. Write to me. Maybe we can FaceTime. Maybe Mom will let us Skype. We can at least text or email." Dallas went on and on, and yes, Reid was pretty sure that was liquid running down his cheek.

It was to the point that Houston was actually trying to push him away. As Reid watched, Houston seemed to shake his head a little, grabbing Dallas by the shoulders and trying to catch his eye.

Reid hadn't had a twin, but it seemed there was some kind of message passing between them.

Whatever it was, he was grateful, because Houston seemed to calm Dallas down some. Dallas wiped the side of his face and jerked his head down.

"Well, I am."

"I'm going to miss you too. I'm sure Mom can be talked into something. Maybe we can even talk them into letting us talk on the phone." Houston's eyes slanted over to Reid who had a brow raised. That was weird.

It was like they were talking about him. "Guys, I'm standing right here."

"Oh? We weren't sure if you were listening," Dallas said.

Reid wasn't used to dealing with them both at once, but he had a feeling something fishy was going on. Their voices sounded like they were reading from a script.

It probably had something to do with some game they'd been playing in the last three days. Maybe Emerson and he had made a bad choice when they'd decided to split them up. It seemed the fairest way to do things, each of them getting a boy for six months of the year.

Maybe the boys were being deprived.

He and Emerson didn't talk much, their emails were short, but maybe this was something he needed to bring up with her.

He didn't look forward to that. The more time he spent talking to her, the more he remembered how much he liked her. It was better to just not. Focus on his own problems, like how he was going to save the farm.

More likely on what he was going to do when the bank took his farm.

"I'll talk to your mother about it."

"You'll call her?" Houston said, with wide eyes.

"No," he said, like that wasn't even something he would consider, because it wasn't. No way. He wasn't calling her. He'd managed to not talk to her at all since the boys had left. Email had been sufficient.

Even when the boys were little, they'd hired someone to fly with them up until they could do it on their own.

"I'll email her about it."

"Oh." Houston's head went down, but his eyes hooked on Dallas's, and they shared another one of those looks.

Whatever they meant, Reid wasn't going to worry about it.

"Well, buddy, you better get on the plane, they're about to call the first group."

Dallas nodded, and Reid walked with him up to the ticket agent, who scanned Dallas's phone before waiting for someone to come and escort Dallas onto the plane.

Reid watched until his son was out of sight, that empty, hollow feeling in his chest expanding like he'd swallowed a balloon. Yeah, this was the worst part about sharing the kids.

Watching him walk away, worrying about his safety, wondering when he'd get there...he hated it all.

Out of sight, out of mind was never true. Not for Dallas nor Houston.

Never for Emerson either.

He wasn't sure there was a day that went by he didn't think about her.

Each day was tinged with a little regret too.

Maybe that was because he could do something about it, apologize, talk to her. Maybe.

But if she wanted him, she could do the same.

And she hadn't.

"Hey, Dad, I have to go to the bathroom." Houston tugged on his arm.

Back home in Cowboy Crossing, it wouldn't be a question. He'd just tell his son to go. But this was St. Louis, and the airport was crowded today. Things were wild at the ticket booth, with a long line of people at the desk, hoping to pick up an empty seat. Two agents spoke with people at the opening of the building. One discussion looked rather heated. He wouldn't be surprised if security was called over that one.

The fuel shortage had been hard on everyone, but it had definitely made tempers flare here.

Once again, he hoped Dallas made it okay.

Dallas could handle himself. Even at ten, the kid was resourceful and unafraid.

Still, it wasn't easy to let your child out of your sight.

Funny that he didn't want Houston to go use the restroom at the airport by himself, but he just put Dallas on a plane alone. Life was not reasonable sometimes.

Most of the time, he waited until the plane took off. Not because he ever thought his kid would get off the plane, just because he couldn't bear to walk away when he knew his kid was still sitting there right outside the building.

Glancing once more at the line of people boarding, he sighed. "Okay, bud, I think it's down this way. We can catch it on our way out."

Houston put a hand on his stomach. "It might take me a while. I haven't felt good all day, and I think I just need to sit down and let everything out."

Reid's brows lifted. Let everything out? Houston had learned *that* phrase from his mother. Maybe it was something the Swiss said.

Whatever. "Okay, kid. We'll get you to the restroom, and you can take as long as you want. I'm not going home without you."

Houston smiled and straightened and took a few steps alongside him. Then, almost as though he was remembering that his stomach was supposed to hurt, he doubled over again and put his hand on it. Maybe the cramp had just let up for a bit.

"Are you sure you're okay? You were acting a little strange today," Reid said, kind of just making casual conversation. Although he wanted to find out if the boys had done anything that he didn't know about. He'd let them play together while he'd done some work in the barn, and he hadn't been with them constantly like he normally was. Typically, they shadowed him while he worked, and then they played. But with both of them there, he let them go off. He didn't like it, because he felt like he missed out, but he also felt like the boys had developed their own secret language in the three days they'd spent together.

Houston's eyes widened, and it was almost like a bit of panic flashed across his face before his look slid into one of complete and total innocence. He nodded, his cheeks puffing a little. "Yeah. Of course, yeah. I'm good. I'm fine. Never been better. I mean, I'm...I'm sad that Dallas is leaving." He shrugged his shoulders and snapped his mouth closed, bending over again and putting his hand on his stomach. "My stomach hurts. That's probably what's wrong." He started walking faster toward the restroom.

It was farther than he thought, or maybe it was the crowds. At any rate, Houston was able to make it to the restroom entrance, his hand still on his stomach as he disappeared inside.

Reid stood outside at the benches, across the aisle from the restroom entrance, pulling his phone out and texting Dallas.

Did you make it on the plane okay, son?

Sure did, Dad.

Do you have your seat belt buckled?

I did.

What do you mean "you did?"

I mean, it was buckled. And I'll buckle it
again, in a bit.

Why can't you buckle it now?

Had he gone to the bathroom?

I texted Mom and told her I was on the
plane.

People walked by Reid as he held his phone in his hand, staring
at it. The sound of them talking about the fuel shortage and the
difficulty in getting flights came vaguely to his ear. He supposed he
should have been paying better attention. He could almost hear
Emerson now, complaining that he hadn't gotten the flight in time
and he'd ended up having the boys for an extra three days.

He couldn't change it now, but he'd have to do better the next
time. The fuel shortage would probably be over by then. Whatever
was causing it, he didn't even know.

He checked to make sure Houston hadn't come out of the
restroom yet, then he looked back down at his phone.

Okay. Good.

Normally he reminded the boys to do that, the last thing before
they shut their phones off—text their mother and let her know they
were on the plane and fine. The seat belt had thrown him off though.
Maybe it was a typo.

He wanted to make sure, so he sent another text.

Did you buckle your seat belt yet?

24

Yes.

Was that for the first time or the second time?

He had to be clear with Dallas. He'd been the same way as a kid. Although he was pretty sure that the airline would not allow his child to not buckle his belt, he still felt it was his duty to make sure it was done.

The first time.

So it's not buckled now?

He waited, tapping his fingers on his phone, impatiently watching for the next text to come through. He wanted to get the seat belt thing straightened out before the passengers were told to turn their phones off.

Normally he was pretty relaxed about these things, and he felt a little bit like an overprotective mother rather than the dad. But he supposed that's what Emerson's and his separation had caused: when he had his son, whichever one he had, he had to be both mom and dad.

It wasn't an easy job.

Finally, a message came through.

No. It's not buckled now. If it were, I wouldn't be able to be in the restroom right now with Houston.

Reid stared at his phone. He tilted his head and read it again.

Was it saying what he thought it was saying?

Dallas was in the restroom with Houston?

But that was impossible, because Houston wasn't on the airplane, and Dallas was. Except, if Dallas was with Houston, then Dallas wasn't on the airplane either. Which would explain why the seat belt wasn't buckled.

Reid pushed away from the wall and power walked into the bathroom. There were two rows, and he looked down the first, which had several people but no young boys, so he kept walking, and there they were, at the far end of the row, heads together.

Houston, always the more cautious of the two, had been keeping an eye out for him. He supposed he knew it was just a matter of seconds until he'd figured out what Dallas had texted him.

Dallas was bent over his phone but looked up when Reid stopped, staring down the bathroom aisle at his boys standing next to the far wall.

There was no surprise on either of their faces: they were expecting Reid to enter the bathroom.

Several men looked at him oddly as he barely slowed his pace, his boots clomping on the floor and echoing on the bathroom walls, his strides long and deliberate.

He tried to keep his voice down, but his neck felt tight and hot. "What are you doing? That was like the only seat on the only airplane and the only flight this week going to Europe." He looked at his phone, trying to remember exactly what time the plane was supposed to take off. If he recalled correctly, it was five minutes ago. "You just missed it."

His boys turned and stood facing him, shoulder to shoulder, their expressions grim but determined. Even Dallas wasn't fidgeting, and Houston had an uncharacteristic mulish look on his face.

Anger had never been an emotion that Reid had had to deal with. Much. Stubbornness, yeah. Pride, he definitely had a problem with that, as evidenced by his wife being in Switzerland for the last eight years and him being too proud to go get her or at the very least ask her to come home.

Not that she would just meekly come. With every second that he left her there, didn't go after her, it made it less likely that she ever would, but that was pride. Because he didn't want to be embarrassed by flying the whole way to Europe to get his wife only to have her tell him he could just shove it.

At one point, he was sure she would come home with him. Now? He was pretty sure she wouldn't.

Still, he didn't really feel anger as he looked at his boys. One of whom was supposed to be on an airplane right now, flying east toward his mother.

"Your mother is going to kill me."

That line made Houston's jaw twitch.

Whatever Reid thought they were aiming for, it wasn't his death, apparently.

Nice to know.

"Do you think she's going to be really mad?" Houston asked hesitantly.

Like, yeah. Double yeah, with whipped cream and a cherry.

"Of course, she's going to be angry. She's already angry that Dallas wasn't there three days ago. She's gonna be extremely angry that he's not on the airplane right now. And most of that anger is going to be directed at me. Even though," he gave his son a look, "I saw you get on the airplane. And you're not supposed to be able to get back off."

Dallas knew better than to smile right now. Reid wasn't yelling, his voice wasn't even raised, although he was using the tone reserved for his kids when they'd done something really, really bad—like miss their flight on purpose. Still, he wasn't quite in the mood to be joking about this. Yet.

"There was a lot going on today, and everyone was pretty distracted. It wasn't hard to get off the plane." Dallas shrugged his narrow shoulders.

Reid pressed his lips together. He believed that. The airplane personnel did their very best, but under the current conditions, with the limited flights and people pushing and fighting to get on, their job was made extra hard, and they also probably didn't normally have to deal with a child who didn't want to be on the airplane to begin with.

Maybe they were used to one who wouldn't sit still, or one who had to use the restroom, or one who annoyed the passengers around them, but one who wanted to get off? Probably not something they were looking for.

Still, he could probably complain to the airline and possibly get a discount on the new ticket he needed to buy....

His eyes narrowed. Another thought came to him. Man, had it been that long since he was young? He'd just figured out this wasn't a spur-of-the-moment action.

He put his hands on his hips. "You guys planned this." His voice wasn't firm; it was like he was asking. Trying to figure out why.

The two identical-looking heads nodded solemnly, freckles on each face going up and down. Freckles they'd inherited from their mother. She'd always hated them, but he thought they were cute.

Now their boys had them.

And why was he thinking about freckles? Emerson was going to be seriously jacked.

"Why?"

The boys looked at each other. Almost as though thinking about some kind of agreement they had. Probably did.

"That's the last time she and I leave you guys together for three days. Holy smokes." He lifted his cowboy hat and ran a hand through his hair. He was in so much trouble. "Why couldn't you have done this on your mother's watch?"

He would have handled it *much* better than she was going to. Not that she usually got angry and threw fits, but she already thought that he was cheating on their deal by keeping Dallas an extra three days. She would probably say something like that in the email she sent—that he was cheating again.

"Because we're together here. Plus, neither one of us likes being in Switzerland. We both want to stay in Missouri."

Reid shrugged. "That's fine by me. But you're going to have to talk your mother into that."

Houston bit his lip and shoved a hand in his pocket. His words came out slowly. "That's what we wanted to do."

Reid stopped in the act of starting to pace and jerked his head around. "What? What do you want?"

"We want Mom to come to Missouri." Dallas shuffled his feet on the floor, still standing beside his brother, but he'd been still for several minutes, and he needed to move.

"How is you missing your airplane going to get your mom here to Missouri?"

"We were hoping you would help us."

"Me?" He couldn't help it; his hand went to his chest, pointing at it. "What am I supposed to do?" He almost added he didn't even want their mother in Missouri, but that would have been way too big of a lie for him to deliver with any kind of straight face or seriousness. He would like nothing more than to see Emerson in Missouri again. In Cowboy Crossing. In his house. As his wife.

Again those two little heads with those splatters of freckles went up and down side by side. Almost like they were in tandem. Probably because they were.

"I can't believe you guys planned this." He shook his head. This time, he didn't resist the urge to pace but walked to the sink, back to the stalls, and back to the sink before finally hooking a hand behind his neck, planting his feet, and facing his boys.

He couldn't lie to them and say he didn't want Emerson in Missouri. But he wasn't going to agree to help them if it was anything that would hurt Emerson or make her even more upset with him. He couldn't take back the past, but he didn't need to continue on the same path.

"What are you guys thinking?"

Dallas's face wreathed into a smile right away, but Houston seemed to recognize it wasn't complete agreement and elbowed him. Dallas tried to get a hold of himself, and Reid tried to bite back a smile. It could be he and his brother Deacon all over again.

"You don't have to do anything bad. You just have to send her an email, telling her that Dallas didn't make the flight and telling her that she needs to come here."

"She's not going to do that. She's going to ask me why. And I can't say because the boys are making all these plans, and I'm going along with it."

"Well, we thought that maybe you could tell her that Dallas locked himself in a room at Grandma's and refuses to come out until she comes. Maybe that would work?" Houston asked, in a scrunched-up kind of voice that said he really didn't think it would but hadn't been able to think of anything better.

"Or I could hide at Grandma's house, and you could tell her you can't find me and tell her she needs to come so she can look for me. 'Cause Mom always finds stuff better than anybody else," Dallas said, like that had been his idea all along. But Houston shook his head, already seeing the holes in that idea.

"I couldn't do that. She'd tell me to call the police." Reid sighed.

Was he even contemplating doing this? Why wasn't he giving his son a hard time, telling him he should've been on that airplane? He should be on his phone right now, trying to see if there was any possible way that he could get a seat on another flight. He should not be indulging the boys in their trickery and deceit.

He wasn't going to engage in any deceit. But he was seriously considering joining in the plan, much to his surprise.

The idea of seeing Emerson again was almost too good to be true.

"I shouldn't even consider this," he said.

Houston's eyes lit up right away, but his face still looked tentative, his mouth opened like he was waiting, hoping to hear the words he wanted.

"I'll call her." He eyed the boys. "I'm not going to lie to her, and I'm not going to deceive her. I'm just gonna tell her exactly what happened, and I'll simply suggest that she should come and get you herself."

He doubted it would work. It sounded stupid and sad when he said it aloud, but he refused to try to trick her.

Probably he should find a flight and book a seat for Dallas and forget this ridiculous idea—the idea that Emerson should come back to Missouri.

"But we want her to stay. We want her to stay for at least..." The boys looked at each other as Houston seemed to be calculating something in his head. He finally spoke again. "At least a month. We need her to stay for a month."

"Need? Why do you *need* her to stay for a month?" Reid asked, emphasizing the "need."

Both heads went down, and both sets of feet shifted on the floor. Houston's hands went behind his back.

"Boys?" It was the most firm thing he'd said. They'd done something pretty awful, and he had been willing to get to the bottom of it. He understood, truly, they wanted to be together, and he understood even that they wanted their mom in Missouri. But need? He didn't get that.

"We're not doing anything bad, Dad. I promise... But we can't tell you." Houston scrunched up his face and tilted his head like he wasn't sure what his dad was going to say.

Maybe if it were Dallas, Reid would have had a different reaction. Not that he favored one of his sons. He just knew one had a propensity toward trouble.

This was Houston. Straitlaced, serious, and never doing anything wrong.

Maybe he was crazy for trusting his ten-year-old, and maybe he was even crazier for considering their naughty scheme, but maybe he was just a little boy at heart.

...Or maybe he was just a man who was still in love with his wife.

He wanted her here too.

Someone coming out of a bathroom stall jostled him, and he looked around. "Let's get out of here. I'll call her when we're in the parking lot. As long as you boys promise that you're going to be honest and aboveboard with me from now on and no disappearing on me, okay?"

"That's an easy promise, Dad. We've been honest with you the whole time. And we don't have any intentions on disappearing." Houston looked him right in the eye, with Dallas nodding alongside of him. His boys had never lied to him, as far back as he could remember, even as youngsters.

"Okay. Let's go. You're not leaving on a flight today anyway."

With the fuel shortage, it could be a week before he got another flight. He'd just lucked into the last seat on this airplane.

The boys shook their heads and followed him out of the bathroom. He kept a close eye on them as they walked out of the airport, believing them when they said that their whole goal had been to get their mother here. But dreading having to tell her that he'd not gotten his son on the flight.

Once they exited the building, Reid pulled his phone out of his pocket and pressed the contact that hadn't changed in eight years.

Chapter Four

Emerson rolled over, groggy but awake enough to know that there was some kind of noise that needed to be stopped.

Her hand came out of the covers, and she felt around. Her alarm?

She hadn't opened her eyes yet, but she was beginning to wake up a little more, and she was cognizant that no, that wasn't her alarm.

It wasn't the oven beeping. Wasn't a fire alarm.

Whatever it was had disturbed her recurring dream. One of her and Reid on their honeymoon.

They hadn't actually taken a honeymoon, because they'd been too poor to afford one, but it was a dream she had constantly.

They'd been in the ocean together, and they were laughing and happy, and she hadn't even gotten to the part where she saw the shark, which was where she always woke up.

But there was this noise she couldn't figure out...

Her eyes popped open. It was her phone. Suddenly she was wide awake and reaching for it. Calls in the middle of the night were never good news. It could be her dad. Maybe something had happened with the factory.

She'd turned in the reports like she'd said, and Sherman was to be going over them.

Had there been a problem?

She grabbed her phone and swiped as she cleared her throat, trying to sound like she'd been up for three hours instead of three seconds.

"Hello?" Yeah. She sounded very businesslike, like she was standing in a boardroom instead of lying in her bed, still shaking off the aftereffects of the honeymoon dream.

"Hello? Emerson, it's Reid."

Her mouth fell open, and her heart shifted. Her breathing stopped. Her hand went to her chest, and sharp needles of pain shot out both shoulders.

That voice.

He didn't need to tell her it was Reid. She knew. As soon as he said hello.

It was the voice from her dream. The voice from her past. The voice from every good memory she had.

She tried to kick her lungs into gear and force her hand away from her heart and back down on the bed. Taking a deep breath, she hoped she could speak in a rational tone.

It had been eight years.

"Emerson?"

The voice again. Not quite as shocking this time. How many times over the years had she dreamed about hearing it? How many times had she begged him in her mind to call? Just call? He didn't even have to come. If he'd just call.

Her breathing was almost under control. It was fast, but she swallowed and tried to dredge up the businesswoman persona that she wore like body armor every day.

"Are you still there?" There was just a hint of irritation in his voice, like he suspected she might have heard that it was him and hung up.

She looked at her phone, though his name would have come up.

She hadn't changed the contact. There would be a heart beside it, too. And his picture. The one they'd taken at their wedding. It had been small, just her dad, his parents, and the preacher.

Not even his brothers or her friends. No one.

They hadn't been able to afford anything bigger. She hadn't cared. He certainly hadn't either.

"Emerson? Can you hear me? Are you seriously not going to talk to me?" This time, there was no mistaking the irritation in his voice. He could probably see the seconds ticking away and knew they were still connected.

She closed her eyes and bit both lips. She could do this. "It is three AM on this side of the ocean, Reid. Excuse me if it takes me a little while to respond, since I was sleeping, deeply and soundly, before I was rudely awakened by your call."

Yeah, that was her haughtiest tone. She didn't know what he wanted, but she figured she needed that advantage. She couldn't talk to him sounding like she'd just woken up. And she definitely couldn't talk to him sounding like she'd just been interrupted from dreaming about him.

Wouldn't he love that? He'd never lifted a finger to do anything to get her back. She didn't need to give him that—that she was still dreaming about him—as ammunition as well.

"Oh. Yeah. I guess it is. I'm sorry. I never thought about the time difference."

Of course he hadn't. He'd never called before. Email or text were what they used to communicate.

She thought she heard him sigh. "I'm sorry. I never had to worry about time zones with emails before."

"It's not a problem, Reid. Not unless you're going to be upset with me for not waking up on your time schedule."

"Of course not. I'm sorry."

Of course he was. He'd said it three times. She wished she could let loose and laugh and tell him it didn't matter. But he'd hurt her and let her go, and she needed some kind of defense against him.

"I assume there's a reason for your call?" she prompted. Just hearing his voice did crazy things to her insides, and she couldn't continue to talk to him. Awake or no.

"Yeah. Of course." This time, there was no mistaking his sigh.

She could almost see him running a hand through his hair and settling his hat back down on his head. He'd done it all the time when he was agitated and upset.

He was probably pacing as well. She almost smiled at that.

She thought better when she was still, with complete and total silence all around her, while Reid needed action, movement, noise, and he thought through it all. She'd never figured out how. But Dallas had inherited all of that, and it definitely made her understand her son a little better to know he took after his dad so closely.

"Dallas was on the airplane today..."

Immediately her heart jumped into her throat, and she threw the covers off her legs and jumped out of bed, like she was actually gonna go do something, although she didn't know what.

"Did his airplane crash?" She put her phone on speaker and started bringing up the news. Was there a plane crash she didn't know about?

"No. No. No, everything's fine. Dallas is fine. Houston is fine. Both kids are fine. Everyone's safe. Everything's okay. There was no plane crash or anything. He's fine. He's right here beside me."

She left her phone on speaker but dropped her hand into her lap and slumped on the bed. Her heart still thumping.

Reid wouldn't have done that on purpose. Not scared her. Sometimes he was completely clueless, typical male, but he would never have hurt her or scared her on purpose.

Two scares in one night.

The first hadn't really been a scare. Hearing Reid's voice had been...nice. Painful, and unexpected, but still nice.

She could recover from the second as well.

Losing one of her children was unthinkable, and with them flying, it was always a thing that was in the back of her head. But they'd been doing it for so many years she supposed she had gotten used to it.

"Okay. Everything's fine. But Dallas is supposed to be on an airplane, and yet he's standing beside you? That's what you said?"

"Yes."

"So there's still a problem. But nobody's hurt. And everyone's okay? Right?"

"Yeah."

His one-word answers were starting to annoy her. She wasn't supposed to have to play twenty questions, especially not in the middle of the night. Still, he wasn't volunteering information, which was unusual, because Reid didn't normally have a problem talking.

Too impatient to wait, she said, "Okay, so we've established the fact that everyone's okay, but there is a problem, because Dallas is not on the airplane where he belongs. Can you elaborate on that?"

She took control because that's what she did. When they were together, Reid typically was pretty easygoing and laid-back, but always moving and the first to jump into something.

They'd always joked about it. She was organized and efficient. Good with money, patient, and didn't make a move until she'd thought things through. He was the exact opposite in every way. They balanced each other out.

She definitely had a tendency to be way too straitlaced, cautious, and boring without him.

Why did she have to start thinking about that? She missed him. She liked the person she was when she was around him. She liked the way they worked together and the fun they had. They might be opposite personalities, but they shared the same values, so underneath the conflict that invariably arose, they were always able to work it out.

"Well, the boys had three days together, and they came up with a plan, because they like being together, and they want to spend more time together."

It seemed like he was emphasizing the together part of that. She didn't say anything. Waiting.

"They seem to be pretty set on not just being able to spend time together but also wanting you to come here."

"So let me get this straight. Dallas was on the airplane, but he walked off, and the boys want me to go there, and you are okay with all of this?" Her voice rose way more than she'd intended with that last phrase. Not quite to shrew level, but a lot closer than she ever wanted to be.

There was a heavy silence. She was being too harsh. Was she?

Maybe she felt like Reid was the dad and should be calling the shots.

Except, that wasn't really it.

She didn't want to go to Missouri because her boys wanted her there. If she were going to go to Missouri, she wanted to go because Reid wanted her. But it sounded like he didn't really care whether she was there, it was just the kids that wanted her.

A person might have thought that after being separated for eight years, she wouldn't give a flip as to where the man wanted her.

Unfortunately, her heart couldn't be persuaded to be reasonable.

Her pulse thumped in her head, and she pushed down anger at the stubborn man she'd married.

Or maybe she was angry at herself, because she was drawn to the idea of going back home, back to Missouri, the state that she loved, back to her rural roots, and the mountains that weren't snowcapped, but were rolling and green and friendly, and not these harsh but very beautiful, very rugged mountains she was surrounded by here.

Back to her small town. Back to her old friends. Back to her high school boyfriend and the husband she still loved.

But she didn't want to go back, not if she wasn't wanted.

"Think the boys are feeling like they'd like to spend some time together. I was kind of thinking about talking to you about it anyway and seeing if there wasn't some kind of way we can amend the way we've been doing things so the boys get to be together. But that's not really what the call is about. I think that it might be best, considering that the boys are so desperate that they would walk off an airplane, that maybe we need to get together and talk about it." He paused, like he wasn't sure what she was thinking. "If it's not too much trouble for you."

Emerson leaned back against the headboard, her head against the wall, looking up at the dark ceiling.

She had everything, all the material possessions she'd ever wanted. More than she ever thought she'd have.

But she wasn't happy. Not with the way her life turned out. Not with the way things were between her and her husband.

She didn't want someone else. Half the time, she wasn't even sure she wanted him—that stubborn, prideful man, although she still loved him, but she couldn't admit that.

Because admitting it would be weakness.

Going to Missouri would show weakness.

"Are you saying you don't think the boys are happy?" she asked, and all the haughtiness was out of her tone. Because more than her own happiness, she had always wanted to do right by her children.

"No. I think the arrangement that looks so good to you and me hasn't been fair to them. And I don't think I saw that until today when I was confronting the boys in the bathroom at the airport and they faced me shoulder to shoulder."

Tears sprang to Emerson's eyes, and her heart clenched. She'd never seen her boys stand shoulder to shoulder, but she loved the sound of that. It was the way brothers were supposed to stand.

"I think..." Reid blew a breath out. "I think they deserve the chance to grow up with each other, even if that's less convenient for you and me." Reid's voice, too, had no arrogance at all in it. Just a humble recognition that what he thought had been the best maybe wasn't.

She admired that. He was stubborn, and the man had more pride than a porcupine had stickers, but he'd also been able to admit that he was wrong.

Most of the time.

She could too.

"Well, we've always agreed that we wanted the best for our children. I'd love to figure something out. But it doesn't need to involve me coming to St. Louis."

"I think it does. No one is hurt, but I think you need to be here."

"What are you not telling me?" Her fingers twisted in the bedsheets. Was there something else? Something he didn't want to say over the phone?

"I've never lied to you, and I've never been dramatic. And I'm not doing that now. I just think you need to come. You don't have to, and I'm not telling you to, I'm just...asking. Emerson, please come home." There was a slight pause before he added quickly, "Just for a month."

Emerson's head came off the wall, and she stared straight ahead at the gaping opening that led to the master bath without really seeing it.

Was Reid begging?

It sure sounded like it. He hadn't mentioned the boys in those last few lines. He just asked, begged, for her to come home.

She thought about the project she was working on. She liked to think she was invaluable in her work.

But Sherman was just as involved in it as she was. Maybe not because of interest, but because he had ulterior motives, with his designs on her. She wasn't blind about that. But she hadn't flattered herself that it was really because of her.

After all, whoever married her would be inheriting the vast fortune that her dad had amassed, since he and his British business partner had gotten lucky with stocks and futures shortly after she and Reid had gotten married.

They'd turned it into a business, a profitable one and a large one with a lot of money now.

She was good at what she did. Even if it wasn't what she'd originally wanted to do with her life, she didn't want to walk away from it or give it up. Even for a month.

In her mind, she pictured her boys standing shoulder to shoulder. They looked just like Reid did at that age.

Reid's tone rang in her head—the pleading when he'd asked her to come.

She wanted to see her boys together. But more than anything, she wanted to see Reid.

He'd asked. She could give a little too.

Sherman could take her place for a while.

For a month.

"I'll need to make some arrangements." With the fuel shortage, she wasn't entirely sure she would get a flight anyway. "I'll do what I can. And I'll let you know if I'm able to make it." She thought about telling him to book a flight for Dallas in case she couldn't, but she'd get on it and see what she could do first.

After Dallas got off the airplane by himself, she wasn't sure how she felt about him flying alone anyway. They were blessed nothing had happened to him. Kids disappeared every day.

"Fair enough. I'm gonna drive home, and I'll watch for an email."

"Okay."

She hung up without saying anything more. Maybe she should've asked to talk to the boys, but...maybe she'd be seeing them both. How long had it been since she'd seen them together? Years.

And she could see Reid. She closed her eyes and dropped her head back against the wall again, fingering her phone and wondering if what she just agreed to was the stupidest thing she'd ever done.

Chapter Five

Reid stood in the airport hall. Familiar, especially since it had been just three weeks ago that he'd been waiting on Houston to come down the hall.

He fingered his cowboy hat, running the brim through his hand unconsciously.

Emerson's plane had landed. She would come around the corner any minute. It had been years since he'd seen her.

His stomach tightened and curled.

It had been years since she'd seen *him*.

Once they'd been best friends, soulmates, and lovers.

Now, what would she see when she looked at him?

The question made his stomach sour. He was in the exact same position now as he was when she'd left.

Beyond that, though, he couldn't stop the anticipation that bubbled up in his chest.

He was going to see her. Talk to her. Maybe touch her.

Man, he'd missed her.

On his left, Dallas bounced up and down and side to side. He hadn't quit talking since they stopped walking, chattering about what his mom usually did, and how she was leaving her business, and how they couldn't use a private jet because it wasn't big enough to fly across the ocean. All stuff Reid had heard before, but he still listened with half an ear, because he loved to hear his boys talk, and in particular, he loved hearing them talk about Emerson.

Over the years, he felt like he'd known her because of the things the kids said about her.

Unlike Houston, he doubted Emerson would be last off the plane. Dallas was definitely the most like him, but Emerson wouldn't lollygag around.

At least not the Emerson he knew.

He doubted, after almost a decade as a businesswoman in her father's company, that she'd be less driven or less commanding.

He'd always liked that part of her personality. Being that he was so easygoing and laid-back, he enjoyed watching her move and shake things.

Or come up with the ideas so he could come along behind her and implement them.

On his right, Houston stood still.

This occurrence—them waiting for Emerson—was unusual and hadn't happened in all the years they'd been separated. He'd only gone three weeks, instead of the regular six months, without seeing his mother before she was walking back into his life.

That familiar feeling, guilt, jerked at Reid's neck. It probably hadn't been the best idea all those years ago to keep their kids from one another and have them go six months without one parent.

But what else could they have done?

Worked it out?

The little voice came into his head. Normally he might shove it aside, but today, he kinda felt like it had a point. They should have worked it out. He could have tried a lot harder.

With that thought in his head, he stilled his fingers, taking his hat and shoving it back down on his head, watching as the people started to come around the corner from the plane that Emerson had been on.

Would he recognize her?

His palms started to itch and sweat. What would he say to her? How would he act?

The last time he'd seen her, she'd had Houston on one hip and a suitcase dragging behind her on the other side as she huffed down the steps of the house he still lived in, got into her dad's car, and drove away.

The next week, she'd been in Switzerland with her dad, his partner and the company they was expanding.

Their disagreement seemed so trite now. Except it really wasn't.

He was in the same sort of problem that he was when she left. Only this time, it was worse.

He'd probably be able to hold onto the farm for the month that she was here and maybe a little while after that. But by the new year, he was either going to have to find a way to pay or move out.

That thought dispelled some of his anxiety. Interestingly.

It didn't matter what she thought of him, because he was still going to be the disappointment now that he had been all those years ago.

And then his eyes widened. The question as to whether or not he would recognize her was answered even before Dallas jumped up and down and said, "Mom! Mom!"

On the other side of him, Houston straightened and waved.

He didn't know where he got the idea that she wasn't classically beautiful. He didn't even know what classically beautiful meant. Maybe because she wasn't super popular in school or something. It had never mattered to him. Not when they'd been best friends, not when they'd become more.

She'd always been beautiful to him.

Now was no different. She wore casual business attire, at least that's what he'd term it, because it wasn't something she'd wear around the farm. And it probably wasn't something she'd wear to church either. Not those beige slacks, with the crease running down the front, and a cool-looking light blue blouse that flowed as she walked with casual confidence. She wore flats. Bracelets jingled at her wrist. Her suitcase dragged behind her, and a bag was slung over her shoulder.

She still wore the locket.

He wondered if the picture in it had changed.

It had been the four of them while the boys were still in the NICU, and she still wore a hospital gown. He was leaning over her shoulder with his arms under hers, and they held one of their boys in each arm, still hooked up to monitors and tubes although neither one of them had been on a respirator.

He had that picture on his nightstand. Framed. They looked young, and in love, and like they had no idea of how very much everything was going to cost.

As it should be, because they didn't.

That had been the beginning of the end.

And now she was walking toward him, a smile on her face, her hand waving at Houston while she mouthed, "hi," to Dallas.

Her honey brown hair fell over her shoulders, and her eyes sparkled. She looked amazing. Better than his memories. Older, of course, but beautifully mature, still smiling, still with a confident carriage and the spring in her step he'd always admired. As her eyes went between the two boys, she seemed to skip over him and skip back over. But then, as her hand dropped, and she continued forward, her chin seemed to notch up just a little, and her eyes gazed at him directly.

The nervousness that had disappeared came back in full force, gripping his heart and squeezing hard, before it burst loose, his heart pounding like it was being chased, and he wanted to run with it, away from her.

Toward her.

Both and neither, and he remained rooted where he stood. Waiting. Searching her gaze, wondering what she was thinking, wishing he had the right to step forward and put his arms around her, pulling her toward him, burying his nose in her hair, and feeling her arms wrap around his waist and her body press into his.

He still hadn't moved by the time she reached them, and she stopped. The boys rushed forward, throwing their arms around her. She put one arm around Dallas while pushing some hair back with her left hand before dropping it and wrapping it around Houston.

She still wore his ring.

He was tempted to look down at his own left hand where his wedding band shone golden and true.

He'd never taken it off. He'd never even been tempted to.

He liked seeing the thick band still on her finger as well.

It didn't mean anything. It couldn't. But unconsciously he knew he'd been looking for it, and there was some kind of soul-deep satisfaction that settled in his chest upon seeing it.

She still had her arms around both boys' shoulders, and Dallas was still talking a mile a minute, but her eyes raised to his again.

Man, he hoped his words came out calm and assured and not as a squeak, which was a distinct possibility the way his throat was pinched.

"Hello, Emerson."

At the sound of his voice, Dallas quit talking and looked at him from where his face was pressed against Emerson's side.

Again her chin did that little notch-up thing, and her lips pulled back in a polite smile. Not friendly, just polite.

"Hello, Reid. It's been a while."

Master of understatement.

Anger flared in his chest. A while? Is that what she called the last eight years? A while?

"Years, Emerson. It's been years. You can get it right." Anger laced his tone. He hadn't even realized he was angry. He didn't know why he was angry.

"You are correct. My mistake." She tilted her head down just slightly, acknowledging his accuracy. Which of course made him feel like a jerk for insisting on it.

A while could be considered years. There was no stipulation on it.

Her tone was more stilted than he remembered, more...upper-crust.

His heartbeat seemed to slow and sink. He didn't want her to change. Not too much. Of course, she had grown older and more mature, as he had. But he wanted the fun country girl that he married, that he'd grown up with, that he'd been best friends with and high school sweethearts with. Who'd been his girlfriend all through college. He wanted her. Not this straitlaced, prim and proper and prissy city-slicker businesswoman that stood in front of him.

Maybe she was disappointed in him too.

The jeans he wore probably weren't ten years old, but they were just like the ones he wore ten years ago. He was still that man. Hadn't changed a bit.

That probably disappointed her.

There was no point standing here. He didn't know what he thought was gonna happen when they first saw each other after eight years apart, but he'd pretty much ruined it with his comment criticizing her.

"Come on. If that's all your luggage, let's get out of here."

His eyes skimmed over her face as he turned, not too fast to miss the brow raised at his brusque tone. What was he supposed to do?

His chest felt tight and small. Too small to contain everything that pitched and rolled inside of it. He wanted to touch her. To throttle her, to run away from her, to hug her with the boys, to wrap his arms around his whole family and have everyone together again.

"Are you hungry?" he threw over his shoulder, taking a quick glance and seeing her walking between their kids, with each boy having an arm around her.

He almost stopped short at the sight of the blissful look on her face. She was feeling exactly what he had been for the last three weeks. It eased some of the pressure he'd been feeling inside, compassion rising up and taking its place.

"No," she said, her gaze landing on him then bouncing away. Her arms tightened around her kids. "I'm not hungry."

Dallas had her suitcase, and it rolled behind him.

If this were a normal time and they had a normal relationship, Reid would have offered to carry her shoulder bag. But despite the ring on her finger that matched the one still on his, he probably didn't even have that right anymore.

It was a long walk to their car. The whole time, he fought the longing to walk beside her, with his own arm around her. To have their boys on either side of them. The way it should have been.

The way it could be still, if you worked at it.

That crazy little voice in his head wouldn't be quiet. He tried to shush it, because he didn't want to hear it nor feel the guilt it produced.

She hadn't looked happy or excited to see him. And he figured whatever had happened between them had irrevocably broken whatever they'd had to begin with.

Chapter Six

Emerson stood at the window watching Reid, her husband—how odd to think of him like that—and her boys walking out to the barn together. Dallas skipped alongside, running and kicking rocks, and just now practicing a handspring. While Houston, more thoughtful, more like her, looked up at Reid and spoke, and Reid looked back down, answering.

Her heart pricked.

It hurt and felt good at the same time. She'd not even known that was possible. On the one hand, looking at the boys that she loved and the man that she'd fallen in love with, and still—much to her dismay—had feelings for, and seeing them together did something to her that she couldn't even put into words. Gave her her own longing that almost made her need to move, but she wasn't even sure what she needed to move to do. Just do something.

Suddenly, Reid stopped and seemed to say something to the two boys, gesturing with his hands, before he turned and jogged back to the house.

He'd filled out since she left. He'd been a young man in his twenties, skinny, muscular, and strong, of course, but not like he was now, with the broadened shoulders and confident carriage.

Her eyes tracked him. How could she not admire him?

The door burst open, and he came to a complete and abrupt stop, his eyes landing on her, before looking a little sheepish and taking another step, closing the door behind him.

"I forgot to tell you you don't have to worry about supper. The boys and I have been making it, and we'll do it again tonight."

It was like he didn't want her to feel at home. Was that it?

Maybe he was just trying to be nice. That was probably it, but the hackles on her neck raised anyway.

"Do you not want me to touch anything in the kitchen?"

His brows shot up. "Um, no." He lifted his hat and scratched his head. "I just thought you might have things to do. We didn't really talk about it or anything."

"Maybe we should have."

Why was she being such a witch? Maybe because she resented the easy camaraderie he had with the boys, and she felt left out.

He fingered the brim of his hat, almost as though her words had made him uncomfortable. Obviously, he'd never thought about it before. "I guess we could do that...now?"

"That's probably eight years too late." She wanted to slap herself. What did that have to do with anything? Why was she being like this?

Because this is where you want to be. Because you just realized how unhappy you've been living across the ocean in that big fancy chalet and being the bigwig businessperson. It was fake and uncomfortable and not what you ever wanted for your life at all. Coming back here showed you exactly what you wanted. And you don't like that it's your fault you don't have it.

Like he could hear her thoughts, he said, "You're the one who left. I've been here all along."

"You know exactly why I left. You did nothing to stop it. And nothing to make it right." She felt her eyes flashing, and her words weren't kind. Why not? This was the man she loved. Had loved. It felt like she still did.

"We could've worked through it together. We didn't need your dad to be involved. We didn't need his money. It was supposed to be you and me against the world. Not you and me and your dad." His eyes had narrowed, and the first flush of anger crossed his face.

She hadn't meant to make him angry. She didn't want to. Or maybe she did. She wanted him to *feel* something. Something like she was feeling. She didn't want him to be happy and content with his life and how things had played out. She wanted him to miss her. She wanted him to want her. She wanted him to *need* her. And it just seemed like he didn't. Like she was the only one who was suffering.

If she was miserable, she wanted him to be miserable too, as unreasonable as that sounded.

"We hadn't been able to work through it together, remember? We spent months trying to figure things out, and you refused every solution I offered. Your solution was to have no solution."

"That's not the slightest bit true. You're exaggerating. We could have worked it out. We could have set up a payment plan."

"And we would still have been paying on that. It was over a hundred thousand dollars, which was more money than either one of us might have seen in the last ten years. Unless something has changed?"

His jaw flexed, and a vein stood out on his forehead. She felt like she'd hit a nerve. She felt satisfaction. She also wanted to go over and put her arms around him.

She wanted it to be Reid and her against the world. Wanted that more than anything. Especially now, because obviously what she'd said had hit him and hurt him.

Even though that apparently was what she'd been aiming for, it wasn't a good feeling to hurt the man she loved.

Why couldn't she stop?

"Nothing has changed. You're right." His words were a little softer, but there was a much thicker wall between them now. There was no easygoing humor in his voice or on his face; it was completely closed off to her.

"Then you're admitting I'm right." It's what she wanted all along. They'd fought and argued and discussed, and he'd never said that she was right. He'd always insisted, in his stubborn, bullheaded way, that things would work out.

They wouldn't. She could see that plainly, and so could he. He just wouldn't admit it.

"No. I'm not. You're not right. You weren't right." His eyes narrowed. "A month might be too long for you to be here."

Oh, that hurt. She straightened her back and put on her most serene business face. "You're right. I don't want to stay for month anyway. I'll be getting a flight out of here within the week."

His head went up and down, although his eyes didn't meet hers, and his teeth grated, like that wasn't what he wanted it all.

Maybe that was fanciful thinking on her part.

She grabbed her black carry-on bag from the table. Not even bothering to grab her purse out of it, she shoved the strap over her shoulder. She walked past him, brushing by without touching.

Definitely she couldn't touch him.

"I've already talked to the Forrester triplets. I'll be there this evening. You guys can go ahead and cook yourselves supper." She put her hand on the doorknob, then turned, giving him her most serious look, even though he wasn't looking at her, just in case he did, because she wanted him to know that she was dead serious. "You get the boys today. But I spend tomorrow with them." With those words, she opened the door and strode out.

———

"You said what to him?" Daisy asked, hesitating as she approached the picnic table with a glass of tea in each hand.

"I know," Emerson said as she put her arms on the table and laid her head down on top of them. What had she been thinking? Instead of making things better, she'd just made them worse.

"I'm sorry, but we can't really blame him for being angry." Violet, the triplet that had become a vet, stroked Emerson's hair gently. Her words were true, but she said them sweetly, almost tenderly. She wouldn't lie to Emerson, and Emerson appreciated it, but Violet didn't want to hurt her either.

"I know," Emerson said again. Of course he was angry. She'd been an idiot. A mean idiot.

"Don't be too hard on yourself. I think the fact that you still have feelings for him is what made you be unkind. You're probably upset because it feels like he doesn't." Holly, who had never left the farm, and who had held things down while Daisy had become a doctor and Violet a vet, patted her arm.

Her words were too astute, and they made Emerson want to squirm even more.

"I don't want to feel anything for him. I don't want to care whether he feels anything for me."

"Unfortunately, what we want and what we feel are usually two different things. You can't just make yourself not feel things," Daisy said.

"Are you sure you're not a psychologist instead of a family doctor?" Emerson turned her head, still lying on her arm.

"In a small town, you're a little bit of everything. Some people even bring their dogs in to me, if Violet's out."

"I bet the insurance company has a heyday with that," Emerson said, lifting her head up and taking the tea that Daisy held out. "Thank you."

"I never bill insurance companies. I had some hairy years there, when everyone had to have insurance, but I don't deal with insurance companies. Period." Daisy took a sip of her tea, seeming cool and unruffled.

Emerson scrunched her brows and tilted her head. "No insurance companies? How do people pay you?"

Daisy lifted a shoulder. "I don't have to have as many people in my office. I don't have to deal with all the paperwork. I don't have to pay someone to do the paperwork. It doesn't cost me as much, so I don't have to charge as much, and people can afford it." She grinned a little. "Stop looking so horrified. It's different, but it works."

Maybe if Emerson hadn't been so wrapped up in Reid, she'd want to talk about that some more. The businessperson in her found that fascinating.

But today, all she wanted to think about was Reid.

"Why aren't you guys at work? You didn't take off just for me, did you?" She'd talked to them several weeks ago when she'd gotten her ticket and told them the day she was coming in.

Violet answered after she took a sip of tea. "Holly's here all the time, along with our parents. Daisy and I each only work four days. But instead of having a regular day off, we schedule alternating days, and some weeks we line them up so that they match and we're all here together, and some weeks we alternate so someone's here with Holly."

"That's why we told you today worked," Daisy said. "We already knew we were all going to be here."

"The corn's not ready to take off yet, and we're kind of between harvests, although we've been getting a lot of vegetables. This is a perfect day, and we're all really excited to see you." Violet shifted the bowl of lemons she'd set on the table earlier, taking a slice and squeezing it into her tea.

In high school, Emerson and Reid had been best friends the whole way through. But Emerson had also had the triplets as girl pals. Even though there was just one of her, being that she was an only child, she seemed to fit in with them, and they joked sometimes that they were actually quadruplets.

"Why don't you just tell him how you feel? I mean, what's it going to matter?" Daisy moved her tea back away from the edge of the table and sat down. "You're going back to Switzerland. Will it matter if he knows how you really feel?"

Emerson put an elbow on the table and rubbed her forehead. "Right now, he thinks I hate him, since I just picked a stupid fight over nothing this morning and acted like an idiot. You'd think I'd be too old to do that. I should have outgrown that years ago."

"Years ago, you were not like that," Violet said seriously. "I'm not sure what brought it on today." She leveled a sharp look at Emerson. "I don't think living in Switzerland agrees with you."

Emerson knew it didn't. It was a beautiful country, and she really did love it. But it wasn't home.

She didn't say any of that to her friends though. They were already pushing her to say something to Reid, and she didn't know what to say. Didn't know what to do.

"You know, back in high school, I thought you and Reid were perfect together. Even through college, when you guys came home and visited, it always amazed me how you two seem to be equal halves of a whole." Holly bit her lip and looked down at her glass, gently swirling the ice so it clinked against the sides. "In fact, that was part of the reason I was never with anyone. I never found anyone that I could be like that with. So comfortable and perfect. I didn't want to settle for something less. I always admired that." Holly tilted her head and spoke sincerely, and Emerson didn't doubt her. Although her mouth hung open. She hadn't realized Holly felt that way.

"You look shocked. Do you know how perfect you two were together?" Daisy asked softly. Tough as steel—Missouri farm girl tough—Daisy had a compassion, and a perfect bedside manner, that befitted a physician.

"I guess I never thought of it." She hadn't. It just felt right and perfect, but she'd never stopped to consider how it looked to others. She glanced down at her hand. "Maybe that's why I never took off my ring. Never even said the word 'divorce.' There's just no one else for me." It was true. No one had even caught her eye. No one compared. No one felt like they fit her. Not like Reid. Not even close.

"Don't you think that's worth working on? Or worth risking something for?" Violet tapped her fingers on the table and took a breath. "I know, if it were me, it's easy to say this is what I would do. But honestly, if I had that, what you guys had? I would guard it with my life. It's more valuable than anything. And I can honestly say that, after being single for so long. You don't find someone who is your perfect partner in every way like Reid is for you. That doesn't just happen. And when it does, you need to appreciate it."

Her words were gentle, but they hit Emerson's heart. She hadn't thought of it. She kept herself busy, immersing herself in the business, and even now she had a whole briefcase full of work that could be done. When she opened her laptop, there would be even more.

All designed to keep her busy so she would not dwell on what she'd lost.

Had she lost it?

Or had she thrown it away?

"I can see where you guys are right. But, it's hard to explain, but once you reach a certain point, to be the one to make that first move... there's so much water under the bridge that you're really risking, at least it feels like you're risking, an awful lot." She bit her lip, wanting them to understand but not wanting to sound whiny. "What if he rejects me? After the way I treated him, he certainly has that right. I would expect it. Maybe if I could have come and we could have had a friendly conversation or two...."

"It's not too late. You're supposed to stay for a month. Have a friendly conversation or two. You can do it. Just build up to it." Holly, with her can-do attitude and her ceaseless energy, seemed to infuse that into Emerson, and she straightened.

But then she slumped. "I guess I didn't tell you how we ended. I'm booking a flight out of here as soon as possible."

All three of the triplets stared at her in horrified shock.

"You mean you're not staying for a month?" Violet asked.

"No. I haven't looked at flights, but I said I was getting the first flight out." Or something like that. She couldn't remember. She'd been so stupid.

"Maybe you'd better look." Holly's eyes sparkled. She laughed a little. "With the fuel shortage, flights might be grounded. You might end up stuck here."

"Emerson," Daisy said sternly. "I do not, under any circumstances, want you to say that you're moving out of his house. Promise me." Daisy gripped her arm and stared into her eyes, almost a glare.

"I'd like to make that promise. But I had absolutely zero intention of saying that I was going to fly out on the soonest possible flight, and while I have zero intention of saying that I'm going to move out, I don't think I can promise. I just...I don't even know what came over me. There was...there's so much emotion, more than I can handle in..."

She couldn't put it into words, couldn't tell them how the pain mixed with the longing and the loneliness and the blame and the guilt and then with their children, and she just...just didn't say what she wanted to.

It came out yucky and bad and backed her into even more of a corner than what she had been in.

She wasn't sure she could get out. She felt like she needed to fight.

"It doesn't even make sense. *I* don't make sense." She put her head back down on the table.

"Of course you do. It's hard. But think about it. Think about what you really want. Or, even better, think about what's best for everyone and what God wants you to do."

"Exactly." Daisy nodded at Holly. "Not just what you want, but what about your kids? What's best for them? Could you make a sacrifice for them? And, more than that, think about what's right." Daisy's eyes seemed wiser than her years. Maybe because of all the patients she'd seen, and the counseling she'd apparently done, since it was a small town and the doctor seemed to do it all.

Emerson nodded. "You guys are right." She took a deep breath. They'd spent enough time talking about her. "So. Why are you guys all still single?" She eyed her friends. "Do I need to go start shaking the bushes in Cowboy Crossing? There's gotta be some single men worth giving the time of day to."

Silence settled down for a little bit, and all the sudden, all three triplets started drinking their tea. Big gulps in some cases.

Emerson laughed. "Sore subject?"

Violet put her glass down. Empty. "Just make up with your husband. Trust us. What you have isn't easy to replicate."

By the time Emerson left the Forresters' house, it was dark and late.

She pulled up the lane. The farmhouse came into view from the light of the harvest moon. The porch light shone brightly—a beacon that let her know she'd been remembered and cared for—but the lights in the house were all off.

Not surprising, since Reid would probably be up before the sun to feed the animals and start the long day of work. They hadn't talked about the farm, but probably nothing much had changed.

She got out of her car and breathed deeply of the harvest scents. Deep earth, spicy leaves, clear, fresh air, the heavy-sweet scent of corn pollen.

The wind crackled leaves and ruffled through her hair.

Switzerland had clean, fresh air and lots of beauty, but she'd missed the farm smells, the comforting feel, and the people who looked at her and knew her, and shared her background, her interests, and her values. That's what her hometown was. Familiar. A support.

It felt good to be home. And not just because of everything she'd been thinking.

She looked at the house, the dark windows, the silent white walls, the decades of families represented in the ghosts that whispered in the wind, where the three people she loved most in the world slept.

Three. Because Houston and Dallas were the loves of her life, but if she were honest with herself, she loved their father just as much.

Chapter Seven

Gravel crunched, headlights flashed, and shortly after that a car door slammed.

Reid should get up, go somewhere else, so Emerson wouldn't know he'd been waiting on her. Not that he'd exactly been waiting, he was just sitting in the kitchen, well past his normal bedtime, and for the last hour had been straining his ears to hear the exact sound he'd just heard.

He wanted to make sure she got home safely.

He'd already texted Deacon twice. Maybe three times. Okay. Four. Since he was the brother that lived closest to the Forrester triplets.

Deacon had probably been in bed. Maybe he'd been up, but he hadn't said. He'd just texted back ten minutes ago and let Reid know that Emerson was on her way home. He'd seen her going out the drive.

Reid had the feeling he should have gone upstairs as soon as he heard the gravel crunching and knew she was home okay.

She probably wasn't going to be happy to know he'd waited up.

And that definitely said more about his feelings than what he wanted to show.

It was too late. The door opened, and a beam from the porch light cracked in a wider line across the kitchen floor before narrowing again then going out completely as Emerson hit the switch.

They'd only lived in this old farmhouse three years before she'd left, and it wasn't exactly rocket science to know where the porch light switch was, but it still made Reid smile to see her hit it the first time.

She froze for just a second with her hand on the switch, as their eyes met across the kitchen, before she killed it.

He could almost see her stiffen and feel her movements slow.

She was angry, no doubt.

The door clicked closed deliberately. And she turned.

He knew he should be bracing for an onslaught, but the way she turned, naturally, the way they'd always done it—without locking the door—made him wonder if she didn't lock her door in Switzerland.

The thought flashed a pang of fear through his chest.

"I sure hope you use locks in Switzerland," he said, without meaning to upset anything at all. Once upon a time, he didn't measure his words with her and told her everything. They'd been best friends before they'd been boyfriend and girlfriend, sharing farm chores and adventures all through their childhood.

Clark had Marlowe who lived right next door, while Reid had to walk over the hill and through the neighbor's cow pasture to get to Emerson's house. Often she met him in the middle. And as they got older, they'd had ATVs and they'd gone on trail rides, meeting somewhere other than the cow pasture.

"You know, Reid, it's funny, but for the last eight years, I've been taking care of myself. No one stays up, no one leaves the light on, and no one gives me a hard time if I do or don't lock my door."

Her voice had that haughty note in it, and maybe someone who didn't know her as well as he did would think she was a snob or trying to put him down. But he knew it for what it was—a defense mechanism. He'd seen her do it in school when she'd been teased, and with his brothers. Somehow, Emerson always felt hiding her happy personality under a veneer of intellectual snobbery somehow made her less vulnerable.

Maybe it did. When people made fun of your veneer, it didn't hurt like it did when they made fun of your soft underside.

She'd never used that mechanism on him, until that last year.

Maybe it was no longer a veneer. Maybe it was the way she truly was now.

His heart rebelled at that thought.

"And there's nothing wrong with me waiting up. Nothing wrong with me wanting to make sure that someone who's living in my house right now gets home safely. I'm sorry, but you'll never convince me that there is."

She put her purse down on the counter, moving in the dark comfortably. "I'm not trying to convince you of anything. I'm simply telling you I'm a big girl and I don't need you to hold my hand. I don't want you to hold my hand."

"I'm not even touching you." Deliberately missing her point, he also didn't say *not that I don't want to*. Despite the hard time that she was giving him and the feeling of his own anger and irritation rising, he would hold her hand. Touch her. Feel the changes—there had to be changes in eight years. There had been in him.

He didn't go toward her though. Obviously she didn't want him, and it didn't matter what he wanted.

He kept his butt in the chair, and his stocking feet propped up on the chair beside him, one elbow on the table, but his eyes tracked her outline as she moved.

"You know exactly what I meant. You don't have to be technical. I can go out, and you can go to bed, and I don't need to come into the kitchen to find Daddy Reid with his disapproving glower waiting for me to show up. Next thing you're gonna tell me is that I missed curfew."

"You missed curfew."

Years ago, she would have laughed. It would have broken any ice that still lay between them, and they would have kissed and made up.

Not tonight.

"Very funny. I'm serious. I can go stay somewhere else. I don't have to be here. And I'm not going to put up with feeling like you're babysitting me the whole time I'm here. I'm an adult, and I don't need you breathing down my neck."

"You accused me of holding your hand, now you're accusing me of breathing down your neck. Seems like you want me next to you. If you do, just say so. You know I won't have a problem with it."

Reid couldn't seem to stop picking on her. He wasn't trying to patch anything up; he was just trying to prod her for the reaction. He could feel her irritation, but he wanted emotion. Anything besides the cold detachment that she'd been showing.

"Whatever." She huffed. "I don't care what you do. I'm going to bed."

"That's the problem with the world today. Nobody cares." The words sounded bitter as they left his mouth, but he couldn't help it. He wasn't talking about the problems of the world. He was talking about their problems. It truly felt like she didn't care. Maybe it was a veneer, maybe it was her acting...but maybe it wasn't.

Regardless, those words finally had the desired effect.

She whirled from the doorway, stomping over and slapping her hands down on the kitchen table, glowering down at him on the other side.

"You were the one that didn't care," she hissed. "You were the one that let me walk away. You were the one that didn't do anything to stop me or to fix the issues. You were the one that didn't care about the bills we had, and the solution I gave, because you threw it all back. If anyone didn't care," she spat those last two words out, "it was you."

She was definitely anything but unemotional, with her heavy breath, the passionate words, and the slight tremble he could feel through the table.

Reid wished the light were on, because her eyes would be flashing and her cheeks red. The way she'd always looked so beautiful to him.

Not that he wanted her anger directed at him, but at least she'd lost that ice princess façade she wrapped around her and pretended was her real personality.

His legs dropped, languidly, and he rose, putting his hands next to hers on the outside and lowering his head until their noses were just an inch apart.

"You can't possibly believe those lies. I cared. That's why I did what I did. It's also why I didn't do what I could have done."

He wasn't angry. Not really. There was just so much caught up inside him. So much that had been left unsaid, so much that had been left without being resolved. He wanted to grab her. Shake her. Talk sense into her. Kiss her. Make her stay. Apologize to her. Beg for her forgiveness.

Being outside today, knowing she was here, in the same country, same town, *in—his—house* had given him a certain buzz all day that even working with his boys couldn't overshadow.

He'd been pulled toward her, wanting to go in, finding and discarding excuses to walk to her.

Maybe he was goading her, prodding her, picking on her, wanting to know that she felt the same. Wanting to know there was some emotion underneath that cool reserve. Wanting her to blurt out that she wanted him just as badly as he wanted her.

Of course she hadn't blurted out any such thing, and as they stood staring at each other, noses almost touching, her breath coming in angry bursts, his slower, with all the longing of the last eight years in it, they squared off in the dim light across the table.

But nothing was resolved.

She slapped her hands down before pushing back. He could feel the air as she moved, smell the scent on her that had matured but not changed, sweet and powerful and a cheerful contradiction to her ice queen exterior.

Before she could say anything, he straightened too. "Where's that fresh-faced country girl that I grew up with? Where's the laughter, unbridled and coming deep from your stomach? Where's my white-water rafting partner and the girl who put in sixteen-hour days baling hay with me? Where is she?"

Emerson had changed, grown up. So had he. But he didn't think he'd changed that much.

Maybe he had.

He'd never stopped wanting her.

He needed to see that she still wanted him. Maybe then, he'd be willing to take a chance and do the things he knew he needed to in order to have any chance of a future with her.

But whatever emotion Emerson had allowed to be displayed was back under tight rein, and she walked gracefully to the doorway of the kitchen.

Stopping for just a moment, she looked over her shoulder. "That was a long time ago, Reid. We've both changed. Let it go. Don't try to drag the past into the future."

She paused for just a moment, but he couldn't get his mouth open before she disappeared into the darkness of the dining room. Five seconds later, he heard the old steps creaking as she walked up them.

He hadn't accomplished anything except to help her fortify her walls.

Feeling like a miserable failure and also feeling like he wanted to chase after her and beg her to do all the things he wanted her to do, he sat back down in his chair, put his elbows on the table, and held his forehead in his hands.

Lord?

He didn't have to say anything more. The answer was right there. Right in front of him. He'd always known what he needed to do. If he did it, he was almost certain to get his wife back.

The problem was the thing he needed to do—swallow his pride—was too hard.

Too hard? How badly do you want her back?

God always knew the right questions to ask, didn't He?

He supposed this was one of those times where Jesus was making an intercession for him with groanings that cannot be uttered, because he had no more words. None.

It was a long time before he pushed away from the table and made his way to his own room.

Chapter Eight

Emerson stood beside the kitchen counter the next morning, bleary-eyed, having not slept well, and having not gotten any of the work she'd brought along even out of her briefcase.

She doubted Reid had any trouble at all going to sleep.

In her experience, she had a tendency to ruminate on things, while he just put them out of his mind.

This was probably the first time he'd thought about them and their relationship since she walked out the door years ago.

It hadn't made him late for the barn work.

He and both boys were already outside.

The coffee quit dripping, and she pulled the carafe out, pouring herself a full cup.

She drank it black.

There were two cups left in the carafe, and she put it back on the warmer. Reid always came in from the barn and drank two cups, with sugar and lots of cream.

She smiled at the memory. He had such a sweet tooth.

He'd always liked her tandy cake. For a second, she was tempted to make one.

Before she remembered that she was angry at him.

Why would she make him a cake?

Because you don't return evil for evil.

She crossed her arms and turned her back on the counter, like she could turn her back on the little voice in her head, the little voice that sounded suspiciously like the Holy Spirit prodding her to do right when all she wanted to do was nurture wounded pride.

How could the Holy Spirit understand? Jesus never had a girlfriend or a romantic relationship.

But He was betrayed. By people He loved. And then He went on to die to save them.

She gritted her teeth. Why had she read so much Bible?

She wished she didn't know that. She didn't like the guilt it produced.

It was much nicer to wallow in self-pity and wrap her anger around her like a self-righteous cloak.

The door burst open, and she steeled herself, not willing to show a soft side to Reid. But it was Houston and Dallas who ran in, slamming the door shut hard enough to rattle the windows and running straight toward her.

She knew she needed to say something about how hard they'd slammed the door, but it was so unusual to have both of her boys wrapping their arms around her waist that she set the coffee on the counter and returned their hugs, savoring the feel of both of her boys in her arms.

They seemed to have so much fun together. Maybe she and Reid should talk about keeping them together for six months, although she didn't want to be alone for six months of the year while her boys were in a completely different country.

You don't have to be.

She didn't want to even hear it.

"Dad said we could do our school tonight while he's at the single dads meeting, and we can help him today, but only if it's okay with you." Dallas looked up at her expectantly with such a pleading look on his face that she almost said yes on the spot.

"He also said," Houston said, quieter and calmer, "that if you wanted to come out and run the grain wagon beside the combine, he would call Uncle Chandler and tell him that he didn't need to bother to come over."

She loved both of her boys equally, but she loved different things about them. She loved Dallas's exuberance and how he looked and acted just like Reid.

But Houston's calmer, more sensitive nature always pulled at her mother's protective instincts, and she didn't want anything to happen to him. She always wanted to protect him, even though he probably needed it less than Dallas did.

Even though she loved her boys, and loved how eager they were to help their dad, she had to squash her irritation at the fact that he'd sent them in to ask about helping him, when they were supposed to spend the day with her.

Except she didn't have anything planned to do. And he'd also offered to have her out helping, too. That's part of what she missed about being on the farm – everyone working together to get things done. Technically, she would still be spending the day with them.

"Dad said you used to do it all the time. He said you knew how. He said you were actually pretty good at it. But he said that maybe you'd forgotten how, since you've been with all the bigwigs for so long."

"Bigwigs?" Emerson asked, annoyance rising in her once again. It seemed to be her default emotion when she was standing in his house apparently.

"That's what Dad said."

There were so many other things she wanted to talk to them about—their school, and the door, and what they were going to be doing to help, because she didn't want them doing any dangerous jobs. But she had to pick on the one thing that really didn't matter but that irritated her regardless.

She put her hand on each boy's shoulder, still squeezing them to her. When she had married Reid, this was what she wanted. There was no point in ruining everyone's day just because things weren't happening quite the way she wanted them to.

She cleared her throat. "Bigwigs or no bigwigs, I can certainly still run a grain wagon next to the combine. I grew up farming, and you don't lose those skills."

She knew her voice sounded haughtier than what she wanted it to, but she couldn't modulate it. Even though Reid wasn't in the room, she felt like she was defending herself against his accusation. Bigwigs indeed.

Just because she was good at business didn't mean she couldn't be good at farming too.

In fact, before she'd left, Reid and she had agreed that he was great at implementing her ideas but he was too much of a risk-taker to make smart decisions. He needed her to modulate his natural tendency to jump in with both feet and run the numbers later.

They'd been a good pair.

They would still be a good pair.

"Does that mean you'll do it?" Dallas asked eagerly. "Really? You'll drive the grain wagon?" He looked around her at Houston. "You were right, Huey. I didn't think she'd do it, but you said she would. I think you're right!"

Houston had a smile on his face, not huge but satisfied.

Emerson didn't want to let him down. Even though he acted more like her, she could see so much of Reid in him. Reid hid a lot of his insecurities with bluster and eagerness, and although he didn't talk nearly as much as a twenty-year-old as he had when he was fifteen or younger, he still had uttered a lot of words, not wanting to let his feelings show.

Maybe that was a man thing; it was definitely a Reid thing.

"You can go tell him that I'll drive the wagon." She patted each boy on the head. If she were going to do that, she needed to get her coffee in her.

"You can tell him yourself, Mom. He's coming in for breakfast. He said if you didn't cook it, he would. And he'd show us how and let us both help. I help whenever I'm here. I can make breakfast almost as good as he can. Dad said I could. And whenever I do it, I put lots of cheese in the eggs, because cheese is my favorite." Dallas stopped to take breath, and Emerson cut in.

"Then let's start breakfast right now. But..." she emphasized the "but" and looked both boys in the eyes, making sure they were paying attention before she continued. "When you walk in the door," she nodded her head toward the door that they'd slammed, "you need to make sure it's shut, that's right. But you need to shut it gently, because if you keep slamming it like you just did, you can break the glass. It doesn't need to be slammed. Understand?" She lifted her brows and gave both of her boys the most serious look she had.

They nodded solemnly.

"I'm sorry, Mom. It was my fault. I was so excited about getting to help Dad and not having to do school this morning—" Dallas stopped midsentence, his mouth open, his eyes widening and looking at his mom. "We don't have to do school first, right?"

Before she could answer, Houston jumped in. "We promised Dad that we'd do it tonight while he was at the single dads meeting. We'll do it right at the kitchen table. We promise." He looked over at Dallas, who nodded eagerly.

"I promise. I'll sit in my seat until it's all done." He emphasized all of his words, but Emerson shook her head.

"You're not going to be able to sit in your seat that long. Don't make promises you can't keep. You'll need to get up and move around. You can probably even do half of your work standing up. And that's fine. I don't expect you to sit the whole time."

Dallas had looked at the ground and kinda kicked a toe into the linoleum. He nodded. "You're right, Mom. I'm sorry. Sometimes I just say things, and I don't think about what they mean."

She nodded. Part of fixing the problem was recognizing he had a problem.

"Good. I'm glad you understand that. It's just something you need to work on. Just like I have things I need to work on." Like swallowing her pride and not getting upset over everything that Reid did. Reading things into what he did that she shouldn't.

She sighed. So much of parenting was looking at herself and realizing that she had the same flaws her children did. Or maybe not exactly the same, but that she still had things she needed to work on. It was so hard to be hard on her children when she had her own areas that were sadly lacking.

Areas that if she could fix, her kids would've had a mom and a dad living in the same house, instead of in two different countries.

How could she scold them for slamming the door and promising to sit the whole time they did their schoolwork when her faults had such bigger, nastier consequences?

She felt like a fraud as a parent.

"Are we making eggs, Mom? Can I crack them please?" Houston asked from her other side.

"Of course. You crack the eggs, and, Dallas, you can get the cheese out of the refrigerator. Along with some peppers and onions, and mushrooms if we have them. We'll make omelets."

She had the vegetables chopped up, and Houston had just poured the eggs into the skillet, when Reid walked in the door.

Dallas had just said something funny, and both she and Houston were laughing when she looked up to see him filling the doorway.

She couldn't help it. Her laugh stopped abruptly.

She also couldn't help that her eyes seemed to get stuck on him.

He wore a sweatshirt, and it stretched across his shoulders. His hat shaded his eyes, but she could feel them on her, see the muscle in his jaw as it ticked back and forth. He'd definitely filled out in the eight years since she left, and she liked it.

She swallowed, blinking and turning back to the stove, trying to remember what in the world she'd been doing. Her breath felt unsteady, and her brain scrambled.

He took his hat off and stepped in, saying to the boys, "Glad you fellas are helping your mom. Maybe she does things a little differently than I do."

"Oh, she does. She's a lot more careful about not getting shells in the eggs, and I'm not to put the cheese in until last, and I like to put it in and stir it up and have everything all gooey, but that's not the way she makes things." Dallas probably would've kept talking, except Reid hung his hat on the peg by the door and walked to the sink, the scent of warm hay and musky animal, and that unique manly scent that reminded her of honesty and courage mixed in under it all, floating by.

It made her wish she could turn around and step into his arms. That she still belonged there. That the years they'd spent playing together, and running around together, and working together, and building their lives together hadn't been wasted.

She'd never been a believer in looking back with regret.

But in order to not look back with regret, she had to make decisions that worked.

She'd made a major mistake.

Even if she could humble herself enough to fix it, he might reject her.

"Mom said she'll drive the tractor. She said she would never forget. No matter how many bigwigs she was with." Dallas seemed to be gaining a head of steam, but Houston cut in.

"She said that she was a farmer before she was a businessperson, and she would never forget her farming skills."

Emerson scraped the vegetables into the skillet and tried to ignore the heat on her neck that she was pretty sure was from Reid's gaze burning into her back.

"Did she, now?" There was a little bit of humor in his tone, but it was also more serious than what she remembered him being.

Normally he came in from the barn with a smile and a joke or a story of something that happened in the morning.

"Well, maybe she brought her work clothes along with her then?" Reid asked.

Emerson's eyes got big. She'd never even thought about what she was going to wear. She'd brought her business clothes along, but she didn't exactly have a bunch of jeans and T-shirts and sweatshirts like she'd normally wear on the farm. Or even a Western button-down.

"I think I still have some clothes that I left here. I can go look," she said, not turning around from the stove but spreading the vegetables over the eggs in the skillet like it was extremely important that they be flattened out completely evenly in just the right artistic arrangement.

"If you want to run up and check, I can finish the omelets." Reid came over and stood close enough to make Emerson uncomfortable. She dropped the spatula and moved away.

"Okay." The business slacks she had on and the loose blouse wasn't going to cut it outside on the tractor.

The boys were talking to Reid as she exited the kitchen.

Why did she have to be so stiff? So formal?

If she let her guard down and joked or at least laughed, or gave Reid an easy look, he would follow her lead.

He might not be in love with her anymore, he might not even like her that much, but she was the one who was putting walls up and stiff-arming him away.

She had no one to blame but herself if there was no easy family atmosphere in her home.

She just didn't know how to get rid of her attitude.

She opened the door to the bedroom that she and Reid had shared before she'd moved out and went straight to the closet where she'd kept her clothes.

She was a size bigger than she was before she had the twins, but she could probably squeeze into an old pair of her jeans. They would work until she was able to run to the store and get some that wouldn't be so tight.

But her shirts were not going to fit her.

She'd grabbed her jeans from the closet and turned. Her eyes landed on the framed picture that sat on the nightstand on Reid's side of the bed.

It was the four of them in the hospital. She had a baby in each arm, wires and monitors and tubes running everywhere. Each of their little arms were taped to a board to keep them from bending them and shifting the needles out. She couldn't even remember which baby was in which arm, but Reid leaned over top of her, his head just above her shoulder and one big arm of his underneath each of her arms like they were holding the babies together.

He was smiling and looked as happy as a man could be.

Unbelievably, she, in her hospital gown, holding babies that she wasn't sure were going to live or die, smiled hugely as well.

It was the same picture she had in her locket that she still wore around her neck.

It represented everything that they'd wanted for their family. Excitement and eagerness and knowing that whatever they had to face, as long as they were together, they would face it and win.

Except, that hadn't been true.

Not even two years later, she'd taken one of the boys and been gone.

He hadn't seemed to care.

At least, he hadn't come after her.

She had no idea that picture would still be on his bedside table.

He had no idea, she was sure, that she still wore it around her neck.

Why hadn't they changed that picture?

She had plenty more pictures of Houston, and just as many of Dallas, but that was the picture she cherished.

The picture of all four of them together as a family. The first one.

Standing there in the middle of the room they used to share, staring at that picture that had meant so much to her, her throat tightened, and she had to bite her lip to keep her eyes from pricking and filling.

It hit her that all the years between then and now were wasted.

But her mind wouldn't allow her to let her guard down long enough to try to turn the ship of her life in a direction that she actually wanted it to go. She felt helpless against the current or the wind or whatever that was pulling her away. And maybe, she'd gone too far to ever turn around again.

She sighed, trying to push those thoughts aside. Yesterday was gone.

She didn't know if she would have tomorrow.

But she could make memories, beautiful memories, with her boys today. Opening the door that led to where Reid kept his clothes, she rooted around until she found a western shirt, one that was soft and worn from a lot of washings. One that she remembered from before she left. She smiled a little, because it didn't surprise her that he still had shirts that he'd worn in high school.

The man hated shopping.

Turning, she put on the too-tight pants, the too-tight T-shirt, and her husband's soft shirt that somehow smelled of him and was way too big but still fit her just right.

She didn't know what he'd think when he saw her in it. She could always say it was the only thing up there that fit, but she really could have worn one of her old shirts. Just like she put on a pair of pants that were too tight but would work.

Somehow, she'd rather wear his.

If he said anything about it, she wasn't sure if she'd be able to admit the truth—that she simply couldn't resist the opportunity to wear his shirt.

Chapter Nine

"Here, Mom. You stand here. I want to stand next to the water container. I'm really thirsty." Houston pulled back away from the bed of the pickup and squeezed in between Emerson and the water container, pushing her closer to Reid, who leaned against the bed of the pickup right next to the cab.

"If you're thirsty, someone could fill up your drink for you," Reid said, watching as Houston shuffled Emerson down.

Emerson's body jerked stiffly, like she was trying to keep from getting any closer than she had to. She hadn't even looked at him most of the day.

Although, to be fair, what she was doing—driving alongside the combine pulling the wagon—took concentration. If she didn't pay attention, the wagon would stop or go too fast and move out from under the chute of the combine. If that happened, they would lose shelled corn on the ground.

He didn't have to explain to her that every piece of corn that dropped on the ground was a piece they couldn't sell.

But now they were taking a break, eating the sandwiches they'd packed, and leaning against the side of the pickup, and he was free to look at her and enjoy it.

She used to wear his clothes all the time, and although it was annoying in some ways, since he'd go to get his favorite sweatshirt, and it wouldn't be in the drawer where it belonged, he loved it in other ways.

Like now. Seeing her leaning against the truck, her cheeks red, her hair windblown, her eyes sparkling as she moved gracefully, though somewhat stiffly the closer she got to him, in his shirt.

Yeah, it was probably a caveman thing, but he definitely liked it.

He sighed and looked off into the distance at the hundred acres that still needed to be harvested. He should be thinking about something else, because she'd been very clear that she wasn't interested in having anything to do with him.

He should be the same way. Except he wasn't.

"It's hotter than I thought it was going to be today." Emerson wiped a hand over her forehead, catching a couple drips of sweat that were running down her temple. "Much warmer than Switzerland."

"Dad says it's a lot hotter than it usually is around here too." Dallas was jumping around the driver side door and accidentally bumped into Reid, shoving him closer to Emerson.

He was able to catch his balance before he touched her, and he turned irritated eyes on his son.

"Remember what I told you in the airport, buddy? About paying attention to where your body is in space, and watching that you don't hit people?"

Dallas nodded his head up and down really fast. "Yes. I'm sorry. I was just trying to hop on one foot, and I was up to two hundred twenty times, and I didn't want to stop and lose my balance, and I knew I was going to run into you, but it was an accident. I'm sorry."

Reid remembered doing the exact same kinds of things. Jumping on his foot and counting, having a competition with himself to see how high he could get. Unable to just stand and eat, even when that was what everyone else was doing.

"You didn't hurt me, you just have to watch. I know you like to be moving all the time, but you have to pay attention to other people."

"Yes, sir," Dallas said, with a sly glance at Houston.

Reid noticed the look. What was up with that? It was that twin speak that they'd started doing since they'd been spending time together.

Maybe if he'd been a twin himself, he'd understand a little more, but it just seemed like they were communicating without words, and he felt left out. Although he also felt like they were saying something important that he really should know.

He hadn't been able to find the words to ask about it yet.

If he were on better terms with Emerson, he'd talk to her.

She leaned against the truck, her head lifted to the breeze, and her eyes closed with her face tilted up to the brilliant blue sky, cloudless and vast.

She loved it here. He was sure of it.

Maybe you could convince her to stay.

That voice in his head was always so annoying.

"We're done eating. Is it okay if we go play for a little bit?" Houston asked, shoving the last of his sandwich in his mouth.

Reid looked at the sandwich in his hand. Normally he had two eaten by the time Houston had a half done. The kid must've been starving.

He looked over in time to see Dallas giving Houston a look that almost seemed like he was asking, "What in the world are you doing?"

Half of Dallas's uneaten sandwich sat on the edge of the truck.

"Doesn't look like Dallas is done."

"Dallas wasn't very hungry today," Houston said, grabbing Dallas's hand and seeming to almost pull him toward the standing corn.

"Are you sure about that?" Reid asked as they got further away. He'd never known Dallas not to eat everything. Sure, he had trouble sitting still while he did it, but he always had a hearty appetite.

"We're sure!" Houston called as they reached the edge of the corn.

"Don't go out of shouting distance," Reid called.

"Yes, sir," the boys called back before they disappeared into the corn.

"That was kind of weird," Reid said, not really making conversation but almost to himself.

He wasn't sure how Emerson was feeling right now.

She'd talked a little bit at breakfast, but she'd been clear that there were walls between them.

"It really is," she said thoughtfully. "Dallas never leaves his food uneaten. Houston sometimes doesn't eat much, but he eats slowly. Now today, Dallas is leaving uneaten food sitting around, and Houston is eating faster than you."

Reid grinned at the way she'd lifted her brow and talked about his fast eating, like she remembered that he'd always eaten quickly.

She'd been much more methodical, chewing carefully and occasionally lecturing him because "chewing is the first step of digestion" and accusing him of skipping it.

There was some truth to that accusation.

He was trying to think of something he could talk to her about, some common ground they could find where they could just talk without antagonism and maybe lose the stilted feeling that still sat between them.

She beat him to it, although she picked a sore subject.

"The farm seems profitable." She didn't look at him as she spoke but gazed out across the field that they'd been working in.

He supposed there were factors that could still affect the price of corn. They'd had an abundant harvest, but it wasn't going to be nearly enough to keep them from losing it.

He didn't say anything about that though, picking something neutral. "It's been a good year for corn."

If she wasn't staying, if she didn't care about him, he wasn't going to confess his desperate financial situation to her.

Why should he make himself vulnerable when she was leaving?

"I told Houston I would talk to you about maybe the boys being able to be together at our houses for a while, two months maybe? Or maybe even just spending the whole six months together. Half the year at your house, half at mine."

"No. I don't want to do that. I thought about it, and it won't work for me." Her words were snippy and short, like there was no room for argument or discussion.

It made him want to take the other side and argue against her, but he kept his mouth closed.

Until he couldn't anymore. "This is a decision that we'll make together. It's not just you saying no."

"We have an agreement. It's been working. We don't have to revisit it."

"Maybe I'm not happy with it anymore. If it's not working, we talk about it."

"Why should we change the thing that's been working for eight years?"

"But it might've stopped working now. The boys are getting older. Maybe they want to spend time together."

"That doesn't matter. We made a deal, we're sticking to it. It's that simple."

"It's not that simple. I threw a suggestion out, you're not gonna just shoot it down, like your opinion is the only one that matters."

"It feels like we're going in circles here. There's no point saying anything more." She shoved the rest of her sandwich back in the bag and walked to the back of pickup, throwing it in the cooler, before walking off in the direction of the boys.

Why did he get so irritated so fast with her?

He never used to.

He wasn't a psychologist. He definitely didn't want to be, but he kinda felt like he got irritated with her so quickly because that was an acceptable emotion. Out of all the emotions that he felt for her, and all the things that ached and ripped in his chest when she was around, that was one he was able to let out.

The attraction that still burned in his heart? Definitely not something he could act on.

The tenderness he felt toward her, when he wanted to take his hands and brush the hair back away from her eyes, was another thing he couldn't act on. Nor the desire to protect her, to keep her from working too hard, even the possessiveness of seeing her in his shirt, and feeling them together as a family, and that longing to actually provide a stable home and family life for his kids.

The idea of having more children.

Simple times on the farm with lots of love and laughter, and the only person he wanted to do that with was Emerson.

Yeah. None of that was acceptable. The only thing he could show was anger and irritation.

Maybe it's the same for her.

Maybe that little voice had a point this time. Most of the time when he heard that little voice in his head, he wanted to slap his hand across its mouth. But...what if it was right?

Want to see? Why don't you? Just try and see if I'm right.

There it was again, asking the uncomfortable questions.

He didn't know what to do anyway. What in the world could he do to see if she actually had feelings for him? Ask her? Like she'd actually admit it.

Reid thought it was better to protect his heart and wait for her to leave. That seemed like the thing that made the most sense. The safest thing.

———

THEY QUIT around suppertime when it started to sprinkle.

Emerson appreciated God's perfect timing. It had been a long time since she'd been out and active all day, in the open air, and she'd forgotten how tired that could make a person who wasn't used to it.

She was definitely ready to go to the house and sit down. Except, somebody needed to make supper.

Normally—before—that was her job. Back when they were first married. Reid worked outside, and she helped him when she needed to, but he did the outside work, and she did the cooking and cleaning.

After their argument today—a stupid argument that she was totally responsible for because she was just being an idiot—she didn't want to fight about who was cooking.

She parked the farm truck in the shed where she'd gotten it that morning and hopped out.

Both of the boys had ridden most of the day with Reid in the combine, and they were waiting for her as she slammed her door shut.

"It's going to take me about thirty minutes to get the animals fed, then we'll come in and give you a hand with supper." Reid stopped a good six feet away from her. His face was blank, but his words sounded sincere, almost caring.

"Dallas and I can feed the animals if you want to go in and help with supper. I know we can do it ourselves." Houston shoved a hand in his front pocket, a posture so like Reid's it made her smile.

Reid had been picking up a wrench and a couple of bolts from the bed of the truck where he laid them earlier, and he froze, lifting his head and tilting it a little like he was trying to figure out the meaning behind Houston's words.

They made Emerson smile. Just like little boys to want to be able to do everything themselves.

She didn't know what all feeding the stock entailed; usually it was pretty simple and straightforward, throwing some hay down, making sure they had water, and counting them to make sure they were all there. Definitely something two 10-year-olds could handle.

She didn't understand why Reid was taking so long to answer.

"I guess you two can do it. Don't forget to check the water. And I want to know how many are there, so count them twice."

Dallas bounced up and down and turned excited eyes on Houston, who seemed more serious and contemplative.

It was kind of odd that Houston was the one to suggest it when Dallas was probably the one who really wanted to do it.

Emerson didn't spend any more time trying to figure it out though, because that meant that Reid was coming in with her, instead of giving her a few minutes to get in the house and prepare herself to keep resisting his unconscious charm.

She'd always loved watching him work. And today had been no different, except somehow he looked better to her now than he did when he was younger. Now he definitely walked with more confidence, a quiet confidence that she admired.

He'd always been dexterous and adept at running machinery, and she'd always loved the way they seemed to work effortlessly as a team.

It had all come back today. And she needed to get away from him for a bit, not be stuck in the house with him.

"Maybe if the boys don't mind, I think I'll go feed too. It's been a long time since I've been around the animals."

"But, Mom..." Houston began, then seemed to not know what to say. He turned to his brother, almost as though he was expecting Dallas to help him out, but Dallas shrugged his shoulders.

Emerson's eyes went between the two of them. Did they not want her around at the barn? As a mom, that made her warning antenna shoot up like a rocket. She definitely needed to be out at the barn with them. What were they doing that they didn't want her to see?

"You boys start walking to the barn, I'll catch up."

They looked at each other, and something seemed to pass between them before they started out to the barn.

"That was weird," she said as soon as they were out of earshot.

"What?" Reid asked, acting like he had no clue what she was talking about. Maybe he didn't.

"They didn't seem to want me out at the barn. Do you think they're doing something they shouldn't be?"

"Like what? There's nothing out there for them to do that's wrong."

"Have they been with anybody who might've given them

cigarettes, alcohol, or something that they have hidden out there that they could be wanting to do with you and me not around?" She really didn't think her boys were like that, especially not at their age, but that was the only thing she could think of.

"Naw. Neither one of those boys are interested in anything like that. They would never."

"Isn't that what your parents thought of you, when you were out racing your pickup at night? That one summer?"

He looked at her, a thoughtful and somewhat guilty look on his face. Yeah, that was the problem with being with someone who'd known you all your life; they knew the bad things you'd done too. Especially her, since they'd been such good friends as well as boyfriend and girlfriend.

"I was seventeen. They're just ten. There's a big difference."

"Maybe. I'm gonna go out though. I don't know what they're up to, but I'm suspecting it's no good."

"You want me to come too? I was kind of getting the feeling they wanted to be able to feed and do everything themselves. Nothing more than that."

"Then you go ahead to the house. I'll go out, though they'll still get to do everything themselves, because I won't help them, I'll just watch, and you can get supper ready." She really thought Reid was right that the boys weren't going to do anything wrong, but she did think they were up to something a little more than just wanting to do the work themselves.

Reid jerked his head, then grabbed the last bolt and walked to his toolbox, putting everything away before he strode to the house. Without saying anything more.

It was her fault things were so strained between them, and it was her fault that her stomach felt sick and yucky.

She wanted things to be better between them, but she wasn't sure how to do it, and maybe she was just afraid of being hurt again.

After spending the day with him, it was hard to put him out of her mind. She wanted to be closer to him, not walking away.

But she tried to focus her mind on her boys and finding out what they were up to. She knew it was something. Maybe it was a mother's instinct, but she was certain that there was something going on.

Walking slowly to give them a head start, she slipped into the barn, cracking the door only wide enough to get in. Looking across the barn floor, she saw Dallas and Houston standing face-to-face, their heads down. For once, Dallas was still as Houston spoke low and fast, using his hands to emphasize his words, gesturing widely, then seeming to emphasize his point with each downbeat of his hand.

Houston acted a lot like her, but he looked so much like his father that her heart skipped a beat. She loved her kids no matter what they looked like, but she loved that they took after their father so much. Having them with her was almost like looking into his face every day. She didn't want to go six months without that. Not in a foreign country, doing a job she really didn't like, and choosing to be alone, because the things that her business associates did after work weren't the things she enjoyed.

She wanted a family to be with. If that was just one boy, then so be it. She enjoyed spending evenings playing games and doing homework and going skiing and taking walks with her son. Whichever one she had.

Dallas said something back, and Houston shook his head, again emphasizing whatever he was saying with hand motions.

She walked forward slowly, trying to catch a little of what he was saying, but it was so low she couldn't hear a thing.

She stepped on a loose board that creaked, and both of their heads snapped up.

Dallas was the first to recover. "Hey, Mom! We were just throwing hay down for the cows. You can help if you want to. Come on over."

She walked closer to the western-facing hole where the rain poured down outside. It had only been sprinkling when she walked over and had let loose in the amount of time since she'd made it to the barn.

They probably wouldn't be doing any harvesting tomorrow, because everything would be too wet.

Maybe she would actually get her business stuff out and start doing some work there. She needed to.

Chapter Ten

Reid stood at the counter, shaping hamburger into patties. Beside him, Emerson sliced an onion. Dallas and Houston set the table and chattered between themselves.

Reid set the patties in the skillet and looked around for a spatula.

Emerson reached over on her side, grabbed it, and handed it to him.

He grabbed a plate and slid it over to her. She took it and arranged the onions on it.

He finished putting the patties in the skillet, pressing them down with the spatula, while she sliced the tomato.

Reaching into the cupboard, he grabbed another plate and set it down for the tomatoes. She took it and arranged the tomatoes in an artistic circle.

Maybe he should go ahead and go to the single dads meeting tonight. He'd been thinking about staying home so they could have some family time, but the boys had spent most of the day in the combine with him while Emerson had driven the wagon alone. Maybe she would like to spend the evening with the kids by herself.

They seemed to love to do whatever he was doing. Emerson might not believe he hadn't monopolized both of them on purpose.

She grabbed the pepper and handed it over, and he shook some on his hamburgers before taking the spatula and flipping them.

"There's a single dads meeting in town tonight I was thinking of going to. Are you okay with the boys?" he asked.

"I think I can handle them just as well as you," Emerson said, taking the pepper from him and setting it down.

His hand paused midair. It seemed like everything he said, she took offense to it.

Maybe she didn't mean to. Maybe she just didn't understand. "I didn't mean that you couldn't, I was asking if you minded if I go."

That was better, he thought. But it would be nicer still if she would give him the benefit of the doubt and take his words in the very best way possible. She seemed to look for ways to get upset rather than ways to give him grace.

That's because her emotions are the same as yours.

He shoved that thought aside. One of these days, he was gonna figure out how to gag that little voice in his head.

"The answer is the same whatever you meant. They're my children, and I don't have a problem watching them."

She reached over, grabbing the lid on the counter beside her and handing it to him. He fitted it on the skillet. Reid leaned over to grab the rolls from the top of the fridge, handing them to Emerson. She turned and gave them to Dallas, who set them on the table.

"I'll plan on going, then." He thought to do it more to be considerate of her, but the way he felt now it was more to just get out of the house.

How were they ever going to manage to live together for a month? Especially if she took everything he said and turned it into the worst meaning possible.

Living together without killing each other, anyway.

He didn't want her to leave though. The idea of her getting a hotel or staying with someone else made his heart beat sickly in his chest.

He was such a basket case. He didn't want to live without her; he didn't want to live with her. And couldn't say anything without offending her.

She handed him the slices of cheese from where they sat on the counter beside her as he lifted the lid off the skillet.

He took them, putting one on each burger and an extra two on the patty she would eat.

If she noticed, she didn't say anything. He always teased her that she liked a little hamburger with her cheese.

Maybe he should have asked if that was the way she still felt, but he hardly doubted that her taste had changed.

Setting the lid back on, he said, "Usually people start showing up in town around seven, although there's really no set time. So I'll just eat, then run up and get a shower. The boys know where their schoolwork is, and I'm only saying that because you haven't been here."

"Thank you," she said, although she sounded almost grudging about it.

"Hey, Dad?" Houston asked. "Dallas and I can do our schoolwork ourselves if Mom wants to go with you."

"Yeah. Mom hasn't been in town yet since she's got here, and she probably wants to go see everything. She hasn't met everybody, and she probably just wants to go with you and check things out," Dallas added.

Reid narrowed his eyes and tried to keep the suspicion out of his voice. "This is a single dads meeting. I'm pretty sure your mom doesn't want to go."

Both boys stood looking at him blinking before Houston said, "Well, a lot of the guys there are our uncles, aren't they? That means they're like Mom's brothers too. So...it's kind of like a family thing. Right?"

His brothers used to go all the time, but they hadn't been going very regularly since they'd all gotten married.

He was married too, of course, but... His thoughts trailed off.

People would probably make fun of him because he was there without his wife when his wife was finally here in the states and actually staying with him. Although they all knew the story. Maybe none of the details.

"No. Not really," he finally said to Houston. "Actually, I don't think any of my brothers were there the last time. Although, with the rain, probably more people than usual will be there."

He lifted the skillet lid, and Emerson handed him a plate. He took it from her, thinking about who might be there and who might not and whether he should go and not really paying attention. Until his fingers brushed hers.

Honestly, the feeling of a small explosion happening between them pulled his attention back fast. He half expected to see lightning flashing or some other kind of electrical arc.

It was so bad he took a step back. There was no way to cover that, to pretend he actually meant to move away from the stove. After all, he was getting ready to scoop the hamburgers out of the skillet.

It took him a minute to realize Emerson had stepped back too, still holding the plate with the tips of her fingers.

He didn't know where her eyes were, but he was staring at the plate like it was some kind of radioactive moon rock. Half shock, half puzzled contemplation that such a thing would be party to such a huge reaction with just his fingers.

Of course, it had nothing to do with the plate, which was just the media that had gotten her hand touching his. Or maybe it was his touching hers.

She'd probably argue with him about it; he really didn't know whose fault it was. Just knew he hadn't been expecting it.

Standing beside her felt natural and right, and exciting in a way when faced with that attraction. But touching her, *that* was a completely different story.

Holy smokes.

It definitely shot the situation to a new level.

One he had *not* been expecting.

He stepped back to the stove, not knowing what else to do except to pretend nothing had happened.

Pulling the plate away from her hand, surprised they hadn't dropped it, he put the burgers on it, not even really paying attention.

"Don't you, Mom?" Dallas's voice came to him, although he wasn't sure exactly what he'd been asking. Or maybe it was Houston that had asked something.

"I do...do what?" Emerson stuttered. He wasn't sure he'd ever heard her stutter before. But he had to smile just a little, because apparently she hadn't heard the question, either.

"I don't know what you think is so funny," she muttered under her breath.

She didn't sound antagonistic, like she had before, and he felt free to mutter back, "I didn't hear the question either and can't help you out."

"I think it was something about the meeting tonight, but I'm not sure," she muttered back.

"Oh yeah." He'd heard that subconsciously and remembered. "I think they said something about you wanting to go anyway."

While they had been talking, the boys had been chatting between themselves.

Emerson turned and said in her regular tone, "It's really sweet of you boys to want me to get familiar with Cowboy Crossing. But since I'm your mother," she emphasized that word, "I think it would probably be best if I just skip the single dads meeting."

He set the skillet on the cold back burner and turned to carry the plate of hamburger patties to the table.

"Well handled," he said, leaning down to her ear and saying it low enough the boys couldn't hear.

It was probably his imagination, but he thought he saw her shiver. Definitely, the pulse in her neck shuddered.

Maybe the voice in his head had a point.

He'd keep that in mind.

He cleared his throat and set the hamburgers down on the table. "We're going to my parents' house tomorrow night." He actually hadn't said anything about that to Emerson, since he'd gotten the text while in the combine and forgotten to say anything, so he turned and looked straight at her. "If that's okay with you, Emmy."

He hadn't meant to use her nickname. The one that he'd used when they were younger. The one that only he was allowed to use. She had insisted, from the time she was about two, that everyone use her full name. She wouldn't answer to any nicknames.

He was the only one that had an exclusion.

He wasn't sure if he still had that or not, but the word was out.

Maybe she hadn't noticed, or maybe that was what was making her fingers tremble as she arranged lettuce beside the tomato slices.

"That's fine. Did your mother tell you what you should bring?"

"I'm sorry. Now that you mention it, she did mention something about macaroni salad or macaroni and cheese." Depending on how hot it was.

She didn't seem upset, and there was no flash of anger in her eyes, so he said, "I was thinking that I could make it if you didn't want to. I guess I should've said something, but with getting the corn in before the rain started, I wasn't really thinking about it."

"We could probably do both. If all of your brothers are going to be there, you're going to need lots of food. I'll check the cupboard to make sure we have all the ingredients. If we need anything, you can get it while you're out tonight."

"Thanks. Love the way your mind works." He hadn't even thought about checking to see if they had all the ingredients.

He wouldn't think about it until he actually started making it. Then, if he didn't have something, he'd just search the cupboards for an acceptable substitute. Once, he'd tried substituting mustard for mayonnaise, and that didn't work.

Sometimes his substitutions were a big fail.

Actually, most of the time, his substitutions were a big fail. But he had never seemed to master the ability to actually think ahead, at least with cooking, and figure out whether he had the ingredients before he started making something.

That's an area where Emerson really complemented him.

One of the many ways, he thought as he realized that, over the last twenty minutes, they'd worked together the whole time they were making hamburgers, without even really thinking about it and without talking either.

Then that attraction, that almost-explosion, that happened between them.

If they could just get to where they could be civil to each other...

Or maybe not civil, exactly. To where they weren't stilted and guarded, like they were afraid they were going to get hurt.

One of them had to let down their guard first.

He wished it could be him.

He wanted to be the leader, but after everything that he had done, and after the way they'd parted, and after the way she was acting now, he figured it was more than likely she would reject him.

"I'm starved. Is it time to eat? Is it ready?" Dallas asked.

Houston gave him a look, which Dallas returned with an innocent shrug of his shoulders.

Reid wasn't sure why they were trying to get Emerson to go to the meeting with him. As she passed behind him with the plates of lettuce and tomato and onions, he turned his back on the boys and said, "Did you notice they were trying to get rid of you tonight? Did you see anything out at the barn when you were out there with them?"

He hated to think that the boys were actually plotting something. Maybe it wasn't bad, but now that she'd mentioned it, his eyes were kind of open to the fact that they were trying to do something. He just couldn't figure out what.

Her voice was pitched low, and she leaned into him. "Yes. I

noticed. But I didn't see anything out in the barn, although they were talking low and gesturing."

She talked in front of him to keep the boys from hearing. Her breath brushed his cheek, and her scent drifted up, and he breathed deep. Familiar, and beloved, and yet new and exciting too.

She was the same Emerson, and yet she was completely different.

He didn't remember being this strongly attracted to her in high school.

Of course they were teenagers, with all the hormones that involved, but this was almost a physical pull that he couldn't resist.

It was all he could do to not take his hand up and put it on her back, drawing her closer to him.

"I think you're right. I definitely think we need to be keeping an eye on them. There is no telling what's going to happen or what they could be plotting. We'll definitely want to be on guard."

"I'll make sure I watch them extra close tonight, maybe walk out of the room and see if anything happens. I'll keep you posted."

"Good idea. If you need me, I'll come straight home. If there's anything going on, we're gonna want to nip it in the bud. We don't want them to get the idea that they can get away with stuff behind our backs."

"Agreed. We definitely need to stick together on this."

"Exactly. Present a united front. We're adults, they're only ten. We can definitely outsmart them."

"Obviously. We've been there, done that, and we know exactly what's going on. We just need to figure out what it is."

He wasn't sure exactly what that meant, but he nodded anyway. Because he was supposed to be agreeing, and they were also conspiring together. He liked that. It felt way better than parenting alone.

He kind of thought that she was saying that they were together and no one could beat them. It was a good feeling.

Chapter Eleven

Emerson stood at the pencil sharpener, sharpening pencils. Not that she was using a pencil, exactly, she just wanted to get a little closer to the boys by walking around the kitchen table and moving behind them to where the pencil sharpener was located on the windowsill.

She could hear them say something about the shed.

There was a shed on the property, and in days gone by, she thought it had been a smokehouse and a place to store meat because there were no windows and the door sealed tightly with a strong lock.

It was the only such building on the property, strongly built and tight.

Hmm, were the boys hiding something out there?

She didn't want to forget this information, so she pulled her phone out and texted Reid.

They're talking about the shed.

She considered just flat-out asking them what they were thinking, and maybe if they had all been together all the time, she would have.

But this was new.

She'd only ever had one child at a time, and they spent pretty much all of their time together. There had never been any of this whispering, and conspiring, and sneaking. If that's what it was.

Maybe she and Reid needed to realize how having two children was different than one.

She didn't want to jump the gun and accuse them of doing anything they weren't really doing, and she didn't want to ask them and alert their suspicions.

She agreed with Reid. If there was something going on, it was best to nip it in the bud.

Her phone dinged, and she looked down.

> Maybe we can check it out later. I don't keep it locked.

She was done sharpening her pencils and walked behind the boys. As soon as she started to move, they quit talking.

She'd figured. Definitely there was something up.

It was nice to have someone to share the parenting duties with. Maybe she hadn't realized how much she'd missed that. She pulled up her phone and texted Reid again.

> I just went behind them, and they quit talking. I definitely think there's something up.

His text came back right away.

> Do you need me to come home?

That was actually kind of tempting. Not really because she needed him, but because she liked it when he was around. Still, she wasn't going to make him leave his meeting.

> No.

She stared at her phone, relieved that he seemed to be taking this seriously. He didn't act like she was bothering him.

Reid had faults, but one of them was not that he was not a good dad. He'd always been very serious about being a good dad. She could admire that. And she also knew that he'd help her get to the bottom of this, no matter what.

Just like they seemed to be able to do supper together, almost naturally, with their different strengths, they could figure this out with their kids.

———

Reid took a drink of his water. Zane had brought sweet rolls that Waverley had made and was somewhat famous for. People flew in from California just to get them.

Reid had already set some back to take to Emerson and the boys.

Loyal, another of Reid's brothers, had brought some kind of twelve-layer dip that was absolutely fantastic. The remnants were still on his plate, along with a few crumbs from his tortilla chips. Clark, yet another brother, had even shown up tonight, and he hadn't come to a single dads meeting in a year or more.

Reid highly suspected the reason all of his brothers were there was because they wanted to know what was going on with him and Emerson. Gossip traveled fast in a small town, and everyone knew that she was staying at his house.

They were definitely fishing for more information. He hadn't answered most of their questions and had been vague about others. Finally, they'd gotten tired of pressing him and were now talking to Andrew, the fire chief and single dad of two boys.

"It's hard to get motivated. It's not like I don't want a wife, I just don't want to have to go through all the work that it seems to take to find and get to know someone anymore. I want someone I really know that I feel comfortable with and that doesn't get mad at me every three seconds." Andrew put a chip loaded with dip in his mouth and crunched down.

Deacon, Reid's brother who also happened to be the pastor at the white church in Cowboy Crossing, nodded in understanding. "It's important to be friends and to marry your friend."

He eyed Zane, who smirked at him a little bit. Zane had started out with a marriage of convenience and ended up falling in love with his wife. They definitely were not even friends when they were married, having met in a truck stop's ladies' restroom where they'd gotten stuck. Definitely an unusual way to meet one's future wife.

But Zane and Waverley had made it work, despite the ten children they had between them.

If the rumors are true, they didn't even know they had ten kids between them when they'd gotten married.

Reid had a tendency to believe those rumors, because he'd heard it from his mom. She made it into quite a story and claimed to be a witness. She never lied.

"We all had to do it. It's just the way it is," Preston said.

Andrew nodded. "I know. But I've already done it. I've been there. As much as I would love to be married again, I just don't want the headache. I don't want to play the game."

No one suggested he was lazy. They all knew, as fire chief, Andrew would go anywhere and do anything to save or help anyone. It wasn't that.

It's just that a lot of work went into dating, and a lot of times it didn't pan out.

"Maybe it's just me, but women nowadays seem to be pickier," Shane said.

Reid nodded along with the other guys, although he really had no clue.

He'd never even thought about dating. Not as long as he had a ring on his finger. And he had no temptation to take it off.

"Aren't you lonely?" John asked.

Andrew lifted a shoulder and didn't say anything. Not that Reid thought he would. Who was gonna admit to loneliness? John must be feeling pretty low to have even suggested it. It wasn't something they normally would discuss. Although probably, his brothers—before they got married—and all the other unmarried men there were absolutely lonely.

Why else would they be here? Especially after working the field all day. They should have gone home and dropped into bed.

But they were lonely.

Except, Reid wasn't. He'd had a great day, and he'd been looking forward to spending the evening with Emerson and the boys. Not lonely.

He thought of the texts she'd sent him, talking about their kids.

It was so nice to have someone to discuss the issues with. Every once in a while, they had communicated back and forth, but not much. That was the most they'd talked in a long time.

"You should get yourself a dog," Preston said to Andrew. "If you're lonely, a dog will help, and they don't talk back like a woman does." He smirked.

There was some general laughter, and some ribbing from his brothers that were married, and a little bit of backslapping.

They were mostly saying that tongue-in-cheek, because no one, least of all Preston, meant to insult women. He was just goofing around.

"You know, you could make a deal with yourself. If you haven't found anyone by Christmas, you'll adopt a dog. It could be a Christmas present to yourself." Deacon spoke again.

Usually when Deacon spoke, people respected what he suggested. Although sometimes he came up with some really crazy ideas. Like the time he suggested they buy Chandler at auction, or more accurately, that they give Ivory the money to buy Chandler at auction.

Reid had to admit, for a crazy idea, that one worked.

Maybe that was why people seemed to give Deacon the respect they did. Because sometimes the things he said were just totally out there, and they still worked.

That, and he was a darn good preacher.

Speaking of preachers, Reid asked, "Have you heard anything from Pastor Wyatt?"

Pastor Wyatt's wife, Lynette, had recently passed away after a short battle with cancer, leaving Pastor Wyatt with eight kids to take care of himself.

Immediately Deacon's face fell, and Reid wished he hadn't said anything.

"I think he's adjusting."

Reid wasn't sure how long it had been. When Lynette had first passed, Reid had their kids over to his house several times, as had several of his brothers. They'd taken turns—watching them to give Gus time to grieve.

Eight kids was definitely a far cry from the one he was used to. Even two was harder than one.

His phone buzzed as someone asked Deacon if Pastor Wyatt was going to begin pastoring a church again.

"No. He's been clear that he doesn't want that responsibility. Right now, he's focusing on his children. I believe he was making custom cabinets in the wood shop on their farm. I think that's the best thing he can do right now—just destress and heal. There were a lot of high-stress days in St. Louis."

Reid knew exactly what he was talking about from the time his boys had spent in the NICU when they were born. He knew exactly how stressful that was. And expensive.

He looked down at his phone.

He was pretty slow at texting, because he didn't do it much. Back when he and Emerson were dating, they emailed some, but they didn't have phones to do it on. It was a matter of getting on the computer and checking their email.

Definitely the new technology changed the dating scene.

Not that he'd done any dating. He was still married. Didn't want to be married to anyone else.

But he could get into this whole texting thing. He liked being connected with Emerson, even while his buddies were sitting beside him.

"So, Andrew, it's a bet. Marry by Christmas, or you adopt a dog." Preston's voice made Reid look up.

"Preston, if you're gonna do that with Andrew, you ought to do it for yourself too. Same thing for you. Marry by Christmas, or you adopt two dogs."

"I'm a cat person myself," Preston said with a cocky grin and a sticky roll in one hand. "Although, I would give cats up forever for sticky rolls." He grinned again before he took a bite, taking half the sticky bun.

"Okay, so you either get a wife and sticky rolls by Christmas, or you adopt two cats." Deacon had his chin lifted in challenge, although there was a lingering sadness in his eyes, maybe because of thinking of Pastor Wyatt who Deacon considered a good friend.

"I guess I might as well plan on adopting cats, because there aren't any women in Cowboy Crossing."

"Maybe you just haven't looked around enough," Deacon said.

Andrew licked his fingers and took a drink out of his cup. "I have to agree with Preston. It's a small town, and we know everyone."

"Does that mean you're declining it? Wife by Christmas, or you adopt two dogs."

"Whoa. I thought it was one," Andrew said, and he didn't even wait to swallow; apparently the idea of two dogs was a little overwhelming.

"Two dogs isn't any different than two boys," Reid said good-naturedly. Although he really didn't know what he was talking about since he didn't have two boys most of the time nor two dogs ever. But his brother Zane did, so he looked over at Zane. "Right?"

Zane grinned and lifted his shoulder. "Boys can drive tractors. Dogs can't."

Zane had never been a big talker, but he got a lot said in few words.

"Good point," Reid said.

"If we were betting people, I'd be taking bets right now, but since we're not," Deacon's eyes gleamed a little, like he was laughing at a personal joke, "we'll just take down names." He pulled out his phone and punched in a few buttons.

There were about fifteen guys in the back room, and they were almost evenly split as to whether or not Preston and Andrew would be married by Christmas.

Reid had been on the side of adopting animals, but he decided at the last minute to cast his vote for marriage for both of them. Why not be optimistic? While he was at it, he made a mental note to himself. He needed to do something, even if it was hard, to try to talk Emerson into staying.

Chapter Twelve

R eid shut his pickup door and watched as Houston and Dallas ran side by side to where their cousins were playing under the big maple tree in the yard. It looked like they were getting ready to start a baseball game.

His brother Clark stood in the midst of them, and his wife, Marlowe, seemed to be directing children to one side or the other.

He grinned as Houston and Dallas wrapped their arms around each other and refused to be separated.

Deacon and Zane were chatting over by the porch, and the women were probably inside, since he didn't see any out in the yard.

No one other than Chandler and Ivory, who were walking hand in hand off in the distance, too far away for Reid to tell whether they were going to the barn or away from it.

Loyal was probably inside helping with food, since he loved to cook.

A little pang of longing stirred in his chest as he watched Chandler and Ivory for just a minute. Chandler's head leaned down while hers leaned up, and he couldn't see it, but he bet they were smiling at each other.

Most of the time, he could ignore things like that and pretend it wasn't what he wanted anyway.

But maybe because Emerson was home and maybe because he figured people were going to be asking him about her, why she wasn't here and where she was and whether she was home for good. Or maybe because just seeing her had made everything that he'd always wanted stir up in his chest and come to the top.

Whatever was the cause, there was definitely a pull and a longing.

He turned his head away and walked toward the porch where Zane and Deacon seemed to be in a serious conversation.

They stopped talking as he approached. He smiled. "Don't let me interrupt. What's up?"

Deacon said, "We were just talking about Pastor Wyatt and Lynette."

"I thought Lynette passed away?"

"She did. That's what we're talking about. Gus is taking it pretty hard."

"I can't blame him. She wasn't sick very long, and she wasn't old. It's a hard blow." Reid shoved a hand in his pocket and looked out over the pasture field that stretched out to the creek. He didn't want to get in a conversation about death and sadness, and he wished he hadn't walked over.

"It sure is. No one thinks he should be happy." Deacon's gaze followed his. "But he knows where she is and that she's happier there anyway." He blew a breath out.

Reid could understand the loneliness, and the need for someone to help with the children, and just missing her.

But the death itself...it was really supposed to be a blessing to a Christian. Why didn't they look at it that way?

"Is he...able to function?" Reid asked. If the man needed help, Reid needed to be ready to give some.

"That's what we're talking about. Maybe he needs some company, some people to talk to. He's said that he's happier just hanging out on his farm and healing, but it seems like he's doing less healing and maybe going the other way a little." Zane put a hand on the porch post and leaned against it, his other hand in his pocket. "I'm not saying the man's not right to be torn up, because I know I would be if anything happened to Waverley." Zane looked up at the house, and his tone was soft, like the thought of losing Waverley could barely be spoken aloud.

"I know what you mean," Reid said.

Zane's eyes shot back to him, and Reid resented the surprise that was on his face. Just because his wife didn't live with him, just because he hadn't talked to her for years, didn't mean he didn't love her anymore. He always had, and he probably always would. He couldn't imagine how he'd feel if she were gone.

Even though she'd been in Switzerland, he always took comfort in the thought that she was over there, waking, eating, sleeping. He thought of her every day. He could see her in the faces of his boys. Hear her in some of the expressions they used, see her touch in his house: the decorations she'd left, the kitchen utensils she'd used, her clothes in the closet. Everything reminded him of his wife.

"I think that might be part of the problem. Pastor Wyatt sees the kids, sees the house, and everything is just too much for him. And he forgets that God's there, that God has allowed this trial, and he doesn't seem to turn to Him for comfort. Instead of thinking about heaven and the reunion there, Gus seems totally focused on what he lost here. I think it's almost turned into a depression type of thing. And I'm not sure what to do about it." Deacon's voice was full of compassion and love. If anyone could help Pastor Wyatt, it would be Deacon.

Maybe that was the conversation that was going through their heads several hours later when they sat around the campfire. The children were out back playing flashlight tag, having bummed every flashlight that anybody had in their vehicles and all the batteries from his mom's house.

The ladies had gone into the house to look at paint samples, since

Ivory was making final decisions on her kitchen in the new house that she and Chandler were building.

Chandler had gone in as well, saying that he needed to supervise the situation and make sure that his kitchen didn't end up pink.

Loyal was putting food away, and Clark and Marlowe, neither of whom had ever grown up, were out playing flashlight tag with the children. Which left Zane, Deacon, and Reid to watch as the fire burned down to embers.

"If you're still worried about Pastor Wyatt, Waverley and I don't mind taking Tinsley, if you want to go see him tomorrow." Zane leaned down, his forearms on his knees, his hands loosely clasped between them. His gaze watched the fire, never leaving it as he spoke.

Deacon nodded. "I might take you up on that. I don't know that he needs to be taken out or just to be reminded that it's okay to grieve, but his mindset needs to shift just a little."

Reid didn't say anything, but he supposed his mindset could use a reset too. Not that he was close to being depressed or anything, but life was short. Eight years was a lot of time to waste. And that's what it was. Wasted. He didn't want to let another eight years go by, and look back on that, and think it was wasted as well.

"Do you really think he's that bad?" Zane asked gently.

Deacon shrugged. "I don't have to tell you that most of the time we don't say the things that we know we shouldn't be thinking to begin with. I just think he's forgotten, or maybe he's not remembering, that a better day is coming."

They all stared at the fire a little bit before Deacon started to sing.

As we travel through the desert,
Storms beset us by the way.
But beyond the river Jordan,
Lies a field of endless day.

It was a song they'd sung a lot growing up, and Zane and Reid had no problem coming in with harmony on the chorus.

Farther on, still go farther,
Count the milestones one by one.
Jesus will forsake you never,
It is better farther on.

Their family had sung a lot together when they were younger. It might not be as natural as breathing, but it was as natural as farming. There was something about singing together that bonded a family.

Deacon started singing again, but it wasn't a verse that should be sung alone, so Reid joined him in harmony.

Oh my brother are you weary
Of the roughness of the way?
Does your strength begin to fail you
And your vigor to decay?

He made a mental note to himself that he wanted to sing more with his boys. Singing was one of the many things his dad had been good at. Singing around the table, in the car, on special occasions when they had everyone over. They'd even taken hayrides in the summer, and he remembered belting out tunes, usually hymns, at the top of his lungs while sitting on the back of a wagon, bouncing down the back roads of their farm. Emerson would remember that.

Farther on, still go farther,
Count the milestones one by one.
Jesus will forsake you never,
It is better farther on.

Deacon began the third verse and Reid thought of how short life was, and the years he'd wasted. He didn't want to get to the end and look back with regrets.

He thought, too, of Pastor Wyatt and the sadness he'd been going

107

through after losing his wife. He could almost hear Lynette's voice in the words as they sang together.

At my grave, oh, still be singing,
Though you weep for one that's gone,
Sing it as we once did sing it,
"It is better, Farther on!"
Farther on, still go farther,
Count the milestones one by one.
Jesus will forsake you never,
It is better farther on.

Chapter Thirteen

Emerson would have had a good time this evening. She had always fit right in with his family. With six boys, they could be a little overwhelming to some people. But Emerson had grown up with him, and she was used to all his brothers. He was sorry she missed it.

Plus, his mom had always liked her. Not that there were too many people his mom didn't like, but she seemed to have a special place in her heart for Emerson. And Emerson adored her. At least she always had.

They carried their mostly empty dishes into the house, with the boys following him, whispering again.

Emerson sat at the table and looked up from her laptop when they opened the door. Her face did not hold animosity, so either she really was okay, or maybe she noticed that he didn't stay long, wanting to get home to her.

They exchanged a look, and he knew what she was thinking without her even saying anything, whether it was her lifted brows or just the slight tilt of her head toward the shed.

"Hey, Mom. We had a great time," Houston said from behind

them as the kitchen door closed. He continued without giving her a chance to answer. "Dallas and I were gonna go out to the shed for a minute or two." He opened his mouth say more, but Emerson started speaking before Houston could.

"You know, I was thinking that was a great idea. I haven't been out in the shed since I've come back. And I've been very curious as to how exactly it's changed in the years I've been gone."

Okay. If Reid were being honest, he was very tempted to snort at this point.

She was not being subtle at all.

The boys were not fooled, although they looked confused, since both of their mouths were hanging open, and their eyes were hanging on their mom like she'd grown a second head. But they didn't look upset or panicked at Emerson going out. If they were doing something wrong, Reid would have expected some protests, at least.

"Okay," Dallas said, almost skipping to the table with the empty potato salad bowl. "Let's go now before it gets any later."

Odd.

Reid met Emerson's eyes across the kitchen. He'd expected protests, not this eager excitement.

Since it was already dark, Reid wasn't sure what the rush was, but since he and Emerson had wanted to see it anyway, they didn't see any point in waiting.

"Dad?" Houston said, kind of timidly, which was unusual, and Reid looked at him.

"Yes, son?"

"Can I see your phone for a minute? Mine had a new update last night, and it's not the same as Dallas's. I wanted to know if you had it on your phone."

"What is it? I can check," Reid said, reaching into his pocket for his phone, even though he was thinking it was an odd time for Houston to be worried about his phone.

"If you don't mind, I'd like to compare, because Dallas didn't notice it at first, and mine doesn't always show it." Houston stood, kind of biting his lip and flipping his phone over and over in his hand. Normally he was quiet but not anxious.

Glad for his policy of never having anything on his phone that his children couldn't see, Reid figured this was probably a good time for him to let the kids see that he wasn't afraid to let them see his phone at any point and didn't have to race to delete anything before he could hand it over.

Emerson got hers out of her purse. "I can check mine. Maybe I have the update, although I don't recall having to update it last night."

"Sometimes they do them at different times, I think," Houston said, eyeing Reid's phone before sliding his eyes to Dallas, and again that twins' speak, that Reid hadn't even known was a thing, seemed to pass between them.

But he and Emerson could do the same thing, so his gaze locked on Emerson's, and he nodded his head, hoping that she got what he was saying—that the boys might not go out to the shed with them if they gave them their phones to look at the updates.

Emerson seemed to understand, because she gave a slight nod of her head, then handed her phone to Dallas while Reid handed his to Houston.

"Your mother and I are gonna go out and check out the shed, since she seems to be so eager to see it, even though I don't think it's really changed in the years that she's been gone, while you guys check out the new updates on the phones."

"Really?" Dallas said with a bit of incredulousness, and he seemed to snatch Emerson's phone out of her hand.

A stern look from Houston had Dallas rocking back on his heels and seeming to try to get himself to be still.

With a last raised brow and squinted eye, Reid turned and put his hand on the doorknob. "Are you ready?"

Emerson gave the boys a very similar look—they didn't seem to be paying attention—and then pursed her lips, nodding. "I am."

If she thought it odd, as he did, that neither of the boys seemed concerned they were going out to the shed, she didn't say anything.

He opened the door for her, and she walked out with him following her.

He didn't say anything until they'd stepped off the porch onto the path to the shed.

"Are you finding their behavior odd?"

She nodded thoughtfully, picking her way across the dark yard. He wanted to take her arm but refrained, unsure if their relationship was on that level.

"I did. I was wondering if maybe they'd moved their stuff, although I don't know when they would have."

"Me either." Reid sighed and took three more steps before he said anything. "You know what, we're not gonna have any lights. I didn't bring a flashlight, and there is no electricity in the shed."

"There's a pole light right outside. We'll just leave the door open. If we see anything suspicious, we can always go back and grab a flashlight at the barn."

"You're right."

They didn't say anything more but walked side by side down through the yard, toward the shed.

Earlier at his mother's house, Reid had noticed the pretty fall evening, the warm breeze that would soon turn chilly with the changing of the seasons, and the smell of a summer full of goodness that had shifted into an autumn of fulfillment.

His favorite time of year really, with all the work of the summer paying off and the food that would feed his family, the town, and the country for a winter. It was always a good feeling to reap a good harvest.

A satisfying feeling.

Even more so with both of his boys and his wife beside him.

There was just something that bonded families together when they worked and played and reaped the rewards together.

Maybe tonight, after the kids went to bed, would be a good time for him to approach the subject with Emerson. They seemed to have gotten along okay at his mom's house, and she seemed to be softening some toward him.

Maybe.

The walls were still there, but they didn't feel as high or solid anymore.

He opened the shed door, and it creaked back on its hinges. It stuck a little, and he had to give it a good yank in order to get it open.

"You can go first if you want to, but I'm willing," he said. It seemed odd to just jump in front of her. After decades of letting women go first, it just wasn't natural to not give her that consideration, as much as he was pretty sure she wasn't going to want to walk into the darkness first. He didn't want her to, either.

Emerson was usually rather cautious, more so than him, and he was kind of surprised that she didn't tell him to go ahead while she waited in the doorway.

Maybe she was more concerned about the children than he thought she was.

He wasn't really worried that they were doing anything seriously wrong. He thought they were probably just being ornery.

But Emerson sometimes had better instincts for this than he did. And he also had a tendency to just brush things aside, since he was a kid once too, and he felt like he had turned out okay.

Emerson, having not been a boy, seemed to get a little more worked up about stuff.

He stepped in behind her, and some of the light was blocked, so he moved away from the doorway.

Right away, he saw things that he wasn't expecting. A dark pile of stuff near the back wall.

It was humped and smooth and nothing like the few tools that he had left in here somewhere. Other than that, the building had been mostly empty.

Nothing moved. That was good. The shed didn't have any holes, and he really didn't think there would be any animals making their home in here.

"What's that?" Emerson asked, pointing to the pile of things.

"I'm not sure," he said, stepping forward carefully, just in case what looked like a heap of stuff was actually something that was alive but sleeping. He didn't want to accidentally wake up, say, a porcupine.

Maybe Emerson had the same idea, because she hesitated, seeming to stare intently in the darkness. "You don't think it's alive, do you?" she asked softly.

Reid supposed it was his job to walk over and find out. "I don't think so. Hang on, I'll check."

He wasn't afraid exactly. Whatever it was wasn't big enough to do any real harm to him.

He moved forward. Emerson moved with him.

It shouldn't surprise him, since that was the way she always was. Not the kind of shrinking violet who would sit back in the corner, waiting for someone else to do the dirty work. She'd always been willing to jump in.

He pitched his voice low. "The shed is built pretty tight. I mean, I haven't checked it for loose boards, but there aren't any holes or areas where animals can get in and out. I really don't think this is an animal sleeping." The closer they got to it, the less he thought it was an animal.

"I wish I hadn't left my phone with the boys," Emerson said from beside him.

"Me too."

The words were barely out of his mouth when the small amount of light that had been coming in shifted, shortening, and then pitch dark descended.

The door slammed shut. But that wasn't nearly as alarming to Reid as the click of the lock after it closed.

They froze. Then whirled, their arms brushing and their shoulders bumping in the dark.

His hand reached out as he said, "I'm sorry. I didn't mean to bump you."

His hand brushed her hair and the soft skin of her neck before he found her shoulder to help steady her. Or maybe to steady himself.

His nerves had been on high alert anyway, and now, the pitch dark and the warm nearness of Emerson stretched them even further.

"It's okay," she whispered, a little breathlessly, as her hand landed on his chest.

Despite the thoughts whirling through his head—why had the door closed? It had been hard to push open and wouldn't have just swung shut. But maybe, more importantly, why had the lock clicked? Despite those thoughts, he was tempted to put his hand over top of hers and hold it there, close to his heart.

It was where he wanted it.

"Pretty sure that was the lock turning after the door shut." He figured he might as well say it.

"I had the same thought," she whispered. Then she laughed. "I don't know why I'm whispering. Obviously whoever shut the door and locked it knows we're in here."

"Mom? Dad?" The voice sounded like Houston.

He bent his head down to where he thought Emerson's ear was. Her scent drifted up, and it smelled like strength and sunshine and that mature woman smell that was both husky and sweet with maybe just a hint of fruit. He almost forgot what he was going to say. So much similarity to the scent he remembered and loved, and yet it was like that scent was all grown-up, too.

"Is that Houston?" he whispered softly, shoving the scent and the thoughts it evoked aside.

"That's what it sounded like to me, too. Do you think Dallas and he...?" Her voice trailed off almost like she was in just as much disbelief as he was that their kids would do something like this...on purpose.

"Houston?" he said in a much louder voice, inserting as much parental authority into it as he could. "This is a cute joke, but you can open the door now."

Emerson's hand was still on his chest, and he pressed it against him, savoring the feel of her touching him, even if it was just through his shirt, and allowing, for just a second, those feelings that he remembered but had buried long ago, and everything they'd meant to each other, to be brought back by that simple touch before he took her hand in his and held it as he walked toward the door. She followed.

"Dad?" This time, it was Dallas's voice. "Is Mom in there too?"

There was a little bit of fear, or timidness maybe, in his voice, which assuaged some of the anger that had started to bubble in Reid's chest.

It was almost certain that their children had shut the door and locked it on them deliberately.

Maybe they thought it was a joke. He could laugh about it if they unlocked the door right now.

But it stopped being a joke if they were going to stand outside the door and taunt their parents.

"We're both in here. And we're ready to come out. Unlock the door."

There was silence on the other side of the door.

If there had been any light at all, he would have looked down at Emerson, exchanging information just by looking at each other.

Maybe since the light had been stolen, but he was more aware of her presence beside him, could almost feel her response to the children as well. Very similar to his. She would laugh at this if they opened the door. She was also on the verge of anger.

They wouldn't allow their children to get away with locking them in the shed for any length of time.

Her hand squeezed his, and he squeezed back. He'd missed that. Most definitely he'd missed having someone beside him, on his side, the way that squeeze meant.

Emerson moved, her head brushing his shoulder, almost like she were tilting her head to try to hear better.

"Mom and Dad?" It was Houston again. He took a deep breath, blowing it out. They had no trouble hearing that, like he was gathering his courage. "I....I'm sorry, but we are not going to open this door."

"Oh yes, you are, son. You're going to do it right—"

Emerson's hand landed on his chest again. Her other hand, because she kept her right hand clasped in his.

His words broke off immediately. Even though he couldn't see her, his eyes searched for hers in the dark.

Her hand lifted off his chest, and in another second, it landed lightly on his lips.

He knew exactly what that gesture meant, but he was more than a little distracted by the feel of her finger on his lips. He wasn't thinking about talking anymore.

He was thinking about nipping her finger.

Grabbing that hand in his, kissing the palm and her wrist. Her wrist had always been very sensitive.

"Dad, hear us out, please." That was Dallas, and the most mature voice Reid had ever heard him use.

"Go ahead, boys. We're listening," Emerson said, but it wasn't in her authoritative, businesswoman voice.

It wasn't even in her "I'm your mom, and you're going to listen to me" voice.

Her voice didn't exactly sound trembling and weak, but from the tone that she used, he had the idea that maybe his touch had affected her. As much as hers had affected him.

"We put some blankets and a flashlight and some snacks and a couple other things in a pile on the floor."

Ah, yes. The pile.

Reid's hand came up as Emerson's finger started to slip away from his lips. He caught it and pressed it closer, kissing it gently before moving her hand up and kissing her wrist, too.

Maybe he shouldn't have. She hadn't indicated in any way that he was welcome to kiss her.

But she should know if she were going to touch his lips that he'd rather kiss her than do anything else.

She didn't jerk her hand away but allowed him to press his lips to her wrist for several seconds.

Dallas spoke again. "We have your phones, but you could have them if you really want them. Because Grandma knows exactly what we're doing, and she and Uncle Deacon are on board with it. Uncle Deacon is actually gonna come pick us up and take us to stay the night at Grandma's house."

"I should've known your mother was involved in this," Emerson said in a whisper laced with humor.

Reid had to chuckle softly. "Yeah. This has her fingerprints all over it. Deacon's as well. For as serious as he looks, he's such a matchmaker."

"Maybe he's forgotten we've already been matched," Emerson said softly.

Reid didn't like the sadness in her voice. It bothered him. He didn't like to see her sad.

"Deacon's annoying, but he almost always has good ideas." It wasn't that long ago that Reid had been thinking that himself about Deacon's ideas for someone else.

It applied to him as well, he was sure.

Sometimes it was just hard to implement ideas other than the ones that one had planned.

"This isn't a funny trick or joke, boys. It's going to get cold tonight, and your mother shouldn't be outside."

He wasn't entirely sure that Deacon and his mom being involved meant what he thought it did.

Until Dallas spoke again. "You and Mom have some things you need to talk about. And this was the only way that Houston and I could figure out how to get you guys to do it. So if you guys have come to a good decision in the morning, we'll let you out. If not..."

There was whispering on the other side of the door as the boys maybe argued back and forth before Houston's voice came through the door. "If not, we'll talk to Uncle Deacon and decide what to do tomorrow morning."

Beside him, Emerson's breath huffed out. He could only assume it was a laugh. One he had to imitate.

There was no doubt that the boys had come up with this idea on their own. There was also no doubt that Deacon, and probably his mom, had helped.

"We should be grateful they're getting Deacon to help them. I bet that's where the blanket came from." He spoke low so the boys wouldn't overhear him.

"And your mom too. That's probably where the food came from."

He laughed outright at that. "I'm sure you're right. And I imagine there's enough food in there to last us for a week."

He was still a little angry at the boys. He didn't like to be forced into stuff. And he didn't like to have Emerson forced into anything either. There was just as much chance that she would back away, not want to have anything to do with him, as there was that she would come around and soften toward him. No one likes to be forced.

"Boys, you can't force people to do what you want them to do."

"I know, Dad. But you and Mom need to talk. And you guys have been avoiding each other."

Reid couldn't argue with that. He was just as guilty as Emerson was.

"We want you guys to get back together. We want to have a mom and a dad who live together. And we want to be able to play with each other and live with each other. You shouldn't take my twin away from me." Dallas again used that mature voice, the one Reid wasn't used to hearing from him, except at the end where it almost sounded like he was pleading.

Definitely he and Emerson needed to talk about the twins being able to be together.

"If these are the kinds of things that happen when you two are together, I think we're pretty smart to keep half the planet between you two."

"I'm sorry, Dad. I really am. We couldn't think of anything else to do. We tried to have you guys together in the evening, and even when we're working, you put Mom in a different vehicle than the one that you're driving. You guys need to spend some time together and get things straightened out."

"Sometimes things just won't get straightened out," Reid said, not unkindly and not real forcefully either.

"Come on, Dad. All you and Mom need to do is talk to each other and work this out. It's not like we're talking nuclear codes. You guys can be big about this, and one of you has to say you're sorry. Or maybe both of you."

He was right, and Reid didn't have any arguments for it. He and Emerson probably could talk this out and come to a mutual understanding and agreement. At least for him, he was willing to give ground, because he knew without a shadow of a doubt that he still loved his wife.

Chapter Fourteen

Emerson could feel frustration coming off Reid in waves. Maybe anger, although he wasn't typically an angry person. She felt the same way, except she also kind of thought that maybe the boys had a good idea.

Reid and she already had plans to ignore each other for the rest of the week, with her going to see friends and him continuing harvesting, and if she helped, she'd be doing something other than being with him.

They could probably spend the entire month she was here completely avoiding each other.

During the three weeks before she arrived, and for all the time she'd been here, that uncomfortable, guilty ball of scratchy wire had turned in her stomach at the most inopportune times.

Guilt, because Reid had been the one to break down and ask her to come. She had, of course, but she hadn't made any moves since then.

She couldn't sit around and expect him to make the first move on everything.

Maybe this was her opportunity.

She just had to get her nerve up.

"Mom, we put some snacks and a blanket and everything that Grandma thought you guys might need for tonight and maybe all day tomorrow in a pile on the floor. There's a flashlight in there too, but I didn't have any extra batteries." Houston sounded like he might be having second thoughts, and Emerson was pretty sure if they were forceful and insistent on getting out, he would let them. Neither one of their boys were mean.

"Okay, thanks," she said. Maybe she should be trying harder to make them let them out, but for some reason, this was looking like a better and better idea to her.

It was possible, she supposed, that Reid felt the same way, because he wasn't insisting on being let out either.

In fact, he'd grown strangely quiet.

"At least now we know what they've been talking about and what they've been up to all this time," she said under her breath to him.

He shifted beside her, still holding her hand, and maybe he didn't even realize it. She kind of thought if he did, he would have let it go.

"Guess that's a relief in a way," he said. "I suppose it's better that they were plotting on kidnapping their parents, basically, than to have a stash of drugs or cigarettes out here."

There was a note in his voice that she couldn't quite identify. Whether it was annoyance, at himself or at their situation, she wasn't sure. Regardless, there was also some humor there, which made her smile.

"I'm in total agreement with that. Although, I don't think this is something we can let them get away with on a regular basis."

"You mean you're thinking about letting them get away with it now?" His question wasn't as incredulous as she'd thought it might be.

How should she answer that question? It was almost like he was asking if she *wanted* to be stuck in the shed with him all night.

She didn't want to admit that she did. That would be giving him way too much of an upper hand. It would let him know that she still had feelings for him and possibly wanted to work things out.

She didn't want to show that much of herself.

What if he didn't return those feelings?

Pride goeth before destruction and a haughty spirit before a fall.

That verse she'd memorized when she was a kid came to her mind, and she recognized the wisdom immediately.

"I know we can insist on being let out. But I kinda think the kids might be right this time. Maybe the adults in their lives haven't been setting the best example." She almost let it go at that, but it wasn't exactly what she meant to say. "Maybe I haven't been setting the best example." There. She kicked her pride to the curb. Or at least some of it.

"Count me in on that too. I haven't been setting any better an example than you have."

"Mom? Dad? Uncle Deacon just pulled in. Are you guys going to be okay?" Houston actually sounded worried now.

It made Emerson's lips lift a little. He had a conscience at least. She wouldn't want to raise a child that rejoiced in someone else's suffering or, worse yet, enjoyed making other people suffer. Although, she knew from the bottom of her heart that the boys were doing it for their own good.

"There isn't going to be anyone else here tonight. Do you think you guys are gonna have enough food? I can go back in and get some more for you if you want me to. Or I was going to give you some games to play, but Houston said that might not be a good idea, because you wouldn't be talking to each other if you're playing games." Dallas's voice ended uncertainly, saying much less than he might normally.

Neither one of their boys sounded overly happy, even though they'd accomplished their objective.

"Hey, bro." A deep voice came through the door. Deacon, Emerson assumed, although it had been a while.

"So you're involved in this up to your eyeballs, huh, kid?"

"I didn't come up with the idea, although I think it's a pretty good one. Your boys did. You can thank them later."

"You could let us out, and we'll thank you now," Reid said, but there wasn't much heat in his words. Whatever hot emotion which had seemed to be coming off him had cooled, and he stood beside her relaxed and almost, if she had to guess, smiling.

"Where's the fun in that?" Deacon asked.

"You're a pastor. You're not supposed to have fun," Reid muttered.

"Oh. No one ever told me that. I'll keep it in mind." There was a pause, and Emerson could just picture Deacon glancing at both boys before he said, "Not."

Giggles came through the door, and Emerson smiled. Her boys would have a good time tonight, if nothing else. Mrs. Hudson would take good care of them. She trusted Mrs. Hudson completely.

"Seriously, you think you guys are going to be good in there? I don't want to leave you if you're truly not okay with this." Deacon's voice was serious, and Emerson found herself praying that Reid would tell him everything was okay.

Reid bent down, and she shivered as a touch, whisper soft, brushed her ear. His lips?

His voice came, close and low. "Emmy." Her nickname from his lips clogged her throat and pricked her eyes. She'd missed the intimacy of a nickname shared only between them. "Are you seriously okay? I know Deacon will let us out if we say the word right now."

Again, it was up to her to admit that she wanted to be here. Maybe it was a little easier this time, although it was also a little more obvious because every hair on her neck was standing up in a good way from the whisper that had vibrated through her ear and sent warm waves down her neck and straight to her heart.

Obvious, because, seriously, what kind of person wanted to be locked in a shed all night?

"I think it might be good for us," she finally said, surprised at how much easier it was to say that the second time than the first.

"I was kind of thinking the same thing." Again that whisper-soft touch sent shivers the whole way to her toes as he pulled away.

It had felt like sacrificing her pride, but when he agreed, it felt more like making the first move to reconcile.

It felt good.

God resists the proud, but gives grace to the humble.

Another verse she'd memorized from her childhood, and hadn't really understood at the time, or made any connections to anything, popped into her brain.

She'd take grace. She could always use it.

"We'll be fine. You guys go ahead and go," Reid said.

"All right. Someone will be around to check on you in the morning, probably not too early though. I think I might want to sleep in. Maybe you will too."

Emerson bit back a laugh at the humor in Deacon's voice. Beside her, Reid moved. Maybe he was chuckling silently.

She didn't really want him to know that she found his laughter compelling. So, she backed away from the door. His hand loosened on hers but didn't let go.

"See you later, Mom. See ya, Dad," Houston and Dallas called through the door.

"Be good for your gram," Reid said before he too backed away from the door. "You're not afraid of the dark...that wasn't something that you've developed since the last time I saw you?"

"No. I think I am going to be cold, though." She wished she had put a jacket on before she went out to check the shed. She didn't think they were going to be out all that long, and she hadn't considered it. The days had been nice and warm, but things definitely cooled off after the sun went down.

"They said something about a blanket. And a flashlight. We can go check out the stash and see what they left us."

"Okay," she said as she followed him over.

They went slowly, dragging their feet so they didn't trip on anything. She wasn't good with measurements, but she guessed that the shed was maybe twelve by twelve? Not huge. But certainly as big as anything they would need.

"Uff, here it is. I'm going to bend down," Reid said, and she knelt with him, pulling her hand from his and placing both on the pile, feeling around. Their hands bumped.

"We had so many adventures when we were kids, but I don't think we've ever been locked in the shed before," Reid murmured.

A gentle smile tugged at the corners of her lips. They'd had fun childhoods, and they'd been buddies for a long time.

It made the stiffness between them now that much worse. How could they let one misunderstanding ruin everything they'd ever had? How had she allowed it to happen?

"I found the flashlight," she said as her fingers felt the hard, round plastic. She pulled it out and switched it on.

"That makes everything nicer." Reid eyed the stuff in the pile as she did too.

There was a small cooler, and he opened it, revealing sandwiches and fruit and bottles of water. There were several blankets and a pillow.

"Just one pillow?"

With the flashlight on, she could see the smile as well as hear the humor in his voice.

"It's not very big either. Maybe you get it half the night and I get it the other half?"

His eyes slanted to hers, and she could almost read in them what he was thinking.

She'd never needed a pillow when they'd been married. He was a back sleeper, and she'd nuzzled her head on his shoulder.

Her mouth opened before she thought about it. "I think your arms might be a little harder now than they used to be."

She wanted to sink into the wooden floor. Why did she turn the flashlight on?

Well, she could turn it off. So she did. Snapped the thing right off. She didn't have to sit there and be embarrassed while he watched her. Because she'd seen the grin that had stretched across his face when she'd said that.

Man. She didn't normally have a problem with the wrong words slipping out. She never had. Usually he was the one that chatted all the time, and she was the one that took what he said and turned it into something they could do, ideas they could implement, or explained where his logic was flawed.

"I think my wife just gave me a compliment on my muscular physique." Yeah, there was definitely teasing in his voice.

"Is that what that was?" Was she flirting?

Not only had she said something she never meant to, but now she was flirting?

"That's what it sounded like to me. I'm not sure why you turned the flashlight off. You can't appreciate me flexing, if you can't see me."

"Maybe I've seen enough for now." Yeah, that sounded a little more like something she would say.

He didn't say any more, but she heard some rustling as he seemed to separate things. "I thought we'd sit against the back wall?"

"Okay." Flicking the switch, she turned the flashlight back on. Hopefully he was too engrossed in moving things around and wouldn't see her cheeks were probably still red.

They were still hot anyway.

Why it even mattered whether he saw or not, she wasn't sure. She'd been vulnerable now several times, and he hadn't pressed his advantage. Maybe she could trust him.

Chapter Fifteen

R eid took the pillow and the blanket and walked over to the far wall, setting them down before turning. "Are you hungry?"

"No. I'm good. I ate while you were gone."

"I'm not the slightest bit hungry either. There was a big spread at my mom's."

"Did you guys have a good time?"

"It would have been better if you'd been there." There was no humor at all in his voice, only sincerity.

"Sorry."

"You don't need to apologize. It's as much my fault as yours. Probably more so." He needed to take responsibility for what he had done. He also figured that he might as well use this time to take a chance.

Not really because of the decisions he'd made at the party, and not even because of seeing his brothers together and happy and wishing that same thing for himself.

Maybe a little because of him realizing that he wasn't guaranteed tomorrow, and he didn't want to waste the next eight years like he'd wasted the past eight.

Honestly, it was mostly because in the twenty minutes he'd been in the shed with Emerson, he'd realized that there was no one else in the world he'd rather be stuck with.

He wasn't sure what that meant, wasn't sure how Emerson felt about it. And he wasn't sure what he would do if she felt the same way but didn't want to live in Missouri.

There was so much between them that needed to be worked out. But he could start with the basics.

Maybe. They had all night. He didn't need to jump into anything serious right away.

"You want to come over and sit down?" he asked softly, but even he could hear the note in his voice that said he wanted her to even though it was a question. She had to choose him.

She answered by coming over, with the flashlight pointed at the floor so it only shadowed her face. She didn't look at him but dropped down, her back to the wall.

He dropped beside her, close but not touching. They were probably not at a point in their relationship where he could put his arm around her, and she'd snuggle into him, although that's what he wanted.

"You know, we've never been locked together before, but we did lock two of your brothers in your pantry. Which ones were they?" Emerson asked.

He'd forgotten all about that until she'd just mentioned it. "Chandler and Loyal. Before Loyal had the fire and lost his son, he was a jokester. I'm sure we owed him. I can't remember what they did to us." He chuckled a little at the thought.

"I remember. Your dad had fifty-five-gallon barrels for apple cider. They put each of us in one of those and sealed the lids."

"Oh yeah. That's right. You almost died. You owe Deacon."

"I sure do. It was like Joseph in the pit, and Judah coming to save him. I mean, you know, his brothers had already sold him as a slave, but Judah had the idea to save him."

"Yeah. Deacon ended up actually saving you. I don't think he got the lid off, but he put a hole in the top."

"Sure did, thankfully. It was a nice big hole, although not one that I could get out of. But one that your dad got pretty upset about." She laughed. Deacon had ended up getting punished for that, although it had been Chandler and Loyal who actually deserved it, since they were the ones who stuck them in the barrels to begin with.

"Dad was so upset he didn't wait to get the whole story but just dragged Deacon off by his ear." Reid was laughing too. At this point in their lives, an extra punishment or two wasn't as big a deal as it was back then.

"If I recall correctly though, Loyal and Chandler eventually got it, then they ended up having to do something for Deacon. Maybe take his work for a week."

"Yeah, I'm pretty sure they had to weed his share of the garden for a month. There was a lot of garden. Deacon made out okay."

"Thankfully, it didn't seem to affect him. I can't even believe your dad believed it to begin with, since Deacon never did anything wrong."

"He was pretty serious about his apple cider."

"Whatever happened to your apple orchard? Shouldn't you be picking apples right now?" Her voice held a note of surprise, like she'd just remembered about their apple orchard.

"There was a tornado a few years ago. It missed Cowboy Crossing but hit Trumbull and devastated the apple orchard. Dad replanted, but we're not getting enough apples to do much of anything with. He couldn't plant the trees until the next spring, and then he was researching a few new planting methods and decided to go with one that took a lot of time to plant but shouldn't take too much maintenance."

"Oh. That's nice."

They were both quiet for a few minutes, probably because they were remembering that their first kiss had been in the apple orchard.

Reid wasn't big on remembering a lot of dates, and he'd forgotten their anniversary more than once, which Emerson claimed showed he didn't care, but he thought all it showed was that he didn't remember.

Thinking back, he supposed Emerson was probably right. If he cared, he would've remembered. He certainly didn't forget his birthday. He didn't forget Christmas, either.

She had cried and said that if it was important to him, he would have remembered. He thought she was nuts at the time.

Looking back, she'd been right.

Actually, he kind of wished he remembered the date of their first kiss. Now, it seemed like something worth celebrating.

"I remember a deep blue sky. The red apples against the green leaves. And we were having a lot of fun picking." He said that soft and low and slow and didn't give any explanation. But she knew exactly what he was talking about.

"September twenty-third." That's all she said.

He closed his eyes. Of course she remembered.

Why didn't he?

If it's important to her, shouldn't it be important to you too?

Man, he'd thought he'd gotten that voice to shut itself up. Here it was bugging him again.

He didn't want to think about guilt, or whether he'd been wrong, or what he could do to fix it. He'd far rather think about how nice that kiss was.

Actually, as he recalled, one kiss had become two, which had become more than he could count. Was he supposed to remember how many kisses there were?

Dumb question.

Just the important things. The things that were important to Emerson. Because she would remember the things that were important to him.

"I remember you tasted like apples." It had been his first kiss. Hers too.

He supposed it'd been a few years by that point that he'd even thought the idea of tasting someone else's mouth was a good idea.

Definitely that day he'd gone about it with more than enough eagerness to rival an entire litter of Golden Retriever puppies.

He snorted.

"What?" Emerson asked, her voice sounding sad.

"I was just thinking I probably wasn't a very good kisser."

Now it was her turn to snort.

"I remember thinking you were pretty good." Her voice was still soft and sad. He wanted her to laugh. But he supposed that memory was bittersweet for her. Same for him. "You really surprised me, because I'd never thought of you like that before. And although I'd touched you hundreds of times, touching you that day was different."

He looked down at the ground, even though he couldn't see anything, and was tempted to squirm. Because he remembered her touching him, her fingernails on his back and the palm of her hand moving over his cheek, which was probably baby soft since he definitely hadn't been shaving at that age.

She hadn't cared. She'd touched him like she was feeling him for the first time, like she admired him, like his skinny teenage body was everything she'd dreamed of.

"I felt like Superman that day." And every day thereafter that they'd been together. She just had that way of making him feel like he could do anything. Anything at all, because she was right there beside him, admiring him, encouraging him, and loving him.

He'd wanted to be all that for her, too. But he'd always fallen short.

Forgetting birthdays. Forgetting anniversaries. Forgetting the day of their first kiss. Even though it meant so much to her.

"I'm sorry I wasn't good enough for you," he finally said. It wasn't exactly what he meant, but it was a start.

"I don't know what gave you that idea, but it wasn't true. It's not true." Her voice held an edge, and her words were almost snappy.

He hadn't meant to break the spell. He could get lost in thinking about those years. Lost in thinking about their kiss. Lost in thinking about how she made him better. Lost in thinking about changing history and making it so he had done the same for her, instead of just taking and not giving anything back.

She might have said it wasn't true, but he knew it was. He could look back and see it just as plain as day.

"That's where you're supposed to graciously say 'I forgive you,'" he said, trying to make it sound funny, but he supposed his voice sounded just as sad as hers.

"There's nothing to forgive."

"There is," he insisted. "I just told you, you made me feel like Superman. That's not an exaggeration. Made me feel like I could do anything. Be anything. Have anything. All because you were beside me, supporting me and believing in me and admiring every single thing I did, no matter how awful it was. When you kissed me, when you touched me, it just made everything better and right."

She started to say something, but he touched her arm, because he wasn't done.

His hand slid down her forearm, and his fingers, hesitant at first, threaded slowly with hers again.

She didn't pull away. She didn't tell him no. And he relished the familiar feel of her hand in his. He'd never held anyone else's hand like this; her imprint was the only one. He'd never wanted another.

"And yet I couldn't remember our anniversary. I forgot your birthday. I forgot to get you a Christmas gift at least twice. I didn't remember the day of our first kiss. And I honestly can't even remember your middle name right now. You used to always tell me I would remember the things that were important to me. I knew that you were important to me. But I guess you weren't important enough, or I didn't appreciate you enough, for me to make sure those days were special. Because they were. Anything that was important to you, if I loved you like I should have, should have been important to me too. Your birthday, your middle name, your favorite color, all of those things should've been things that I knew. And I'm saying I'm sorry."

He could hear the little crackle as her head moved back and forth across the wall behind her.

"No. No. Just stop. Those dates don't matter. I fussed about it, you're right. And yeah, I think our anniversary is special, and I like to celebrate it. But it was pretty rude of me to expect you to like the same things I did. Maybe you don't like anniversary celebrations."

"I never forgot my own birthday. I like birthday celebrations on my day. I should've done the same for you."

"It doesn't matter."

"It does."

"It doesn't because—"

It was her turn to touch him, with soft fingers that ran down the inside of his forearm while she held his other hand. Those fingers rested there while he was quiet. Burning but soothing at the same time.

Reid's heart tripped. It was the touch he remembered.

"You looked at me like I was the most beautiful woman in the world. You never looked at anyone else. There was never a question in anyone's mind who you were with and who you wanted to be with. I remember a couple of times you were given a lab partner that wasn't me, and I think everyone hated to be partnered with you, because all you did was stare at me. Not that I wanted anyone else to feel bad, because I didn't, but I loved that the whole world knew exactly who you wanted to be with." She shifted in the darkness, maybe shrugging. "It didn't matter that you forgot my birthday. You wanted to be with me just as bad on that day, even if you didn't know what day it was, as you did every other day. It would have been different if I never knew who you were with, or if I doubted whether I was the one that you like the best." Her fingers twitched in his hand. "There was never any doubt."

She was right about that. They'd never really talked about it, but there had never been anyone he'd rather be with. She was the only one. If he couldn't have her, he didn't want anyone.

Despite the lonely nights, the cold bed, the empty seat beside him at the dinner table. Despite the longing in his heart as he watched other people holding hands and laughing together.

He was never tempted to find anyone else. No one else would fit him like Emerson did. He knew it without even searching.

"You're so beautiful to me. I couldn't stop looking at you."

She laughed. "You're the only person in the world that thinks I'm beautiful."

"That's because you are."

There was still a smile in her voice as she said, "I could tell you all of my flaws right now. No one thinks I'm beautiful. I probably wouldn't even pass for pretty. But it doesn't matter when I'm with you, because you make me feel beautiful."

"I have no idea what you're talking about. Flaws?"

"The freckles on my nose? You forget about those?"

"I love those. They give your face character. I love looking at them. I love that our boys have those same ones. I see the freckles on their face, and it just reminds me of you. It makes me smile, because I love them on you."

She snorted, maybe in disbelief. "My nose is crooked. My eyebrows aren't arched the right way, and my face looks like an apple with no cheekbones."

"I like apples." He caught that husky tone of his voice. Maybe she did too, because no one could talk about apples without them going back to the apple orchard and their kiss. "Northern Spy are my favorite."

Now there was no doubt she knew what he was thinking about. Because that's the kind of apple they'd been picking when they stopped to take a break—at the base of one of the Northern Spy trees —and had kissed for the first time. A really long time.

"I can see the word 'apple' distracts you. Forget that. My face looks like a pear."

"No. I think it looks like an apple. And it's beautiful." His words were soft and sweet. "I know your nose is crooked, and I know *why* your nose is crooked, and I love it. And I, don't get mad at me, have never noticed your eyebrows before. Seriously? People look at these things?"

"Of course they do. Mine aren't properly arched. They arch out toward the edges instead of slightly in the middle. It looks hideous. And it doesn't matter how much I try to shape them, they never look the way they're supposed to. And it gives my whole face an out of kilter awkwardness that's just disgustingly ugly."

"Whoa. Hold up." He came up from the wall and leaned over. "Please don't say you're ugly. That's not true. Not the slightest bit true. It kinda makes me mad to hear it, even if it's you saying it."

"I'm sorry. I don't really believe that, but seriously, my eyebrows are hideous."

His hand tapped around, across her leg, which he didn't exactly mean to feel, but he did, and it was softer than he remembered. His hand was tempted to linger, but he was looking for the flashlight.

"Here it is." He snapped it on. Pointing it at the ceiling, he stared at her face. "You broke your nose when you tried to go out the bus door before the bus driver opened it, and you ended up running into the door, and then falling out of the bus, and nosediving into the cement sidewalk outside. That was the most blood I've ever seen anywhere, apart from butchering."

"I still can't believe they let you go with me to the hospital. I think we were only in sixth grade."

"Yeah. That was pretty amazing. I guess that's the cool thing about going to a country school."

"Maybe that's the cool thing about having your mother leave your father and the whole town knowing it and feeling bad for you. So they let your best friend come along to the emergency room, where they put two stitches in my lip and told me to take it easy for a while."

"They gave you a really cool ice bag too."

"I'm pretty sure it was a catheter bag that they cut the end off of and filled with ice from the vending machine down the hall," Emerson said dryly.

"Like I said, it was cool."

"Maybe to you."

"Definitely. The hospital was small, understaffed, and short on funds. But I didn't mind because I was getting out of school and because I was with my best friend."

"They closed it not long after that."

"Yeah. And turned it into senior living apartments. Too bad, because I had some pretty good memories there. Your nose was about six times its original size, and with that catheter bag, you were like the coolest kid on the block. And you were my best friend."

"Would you stop trying to make me feel better? My nose is crooked, and it's almost as hideous as my eyebrows."

"I love your nose, because I lived the story that goes along with it. I love your eyebrows, now that I can see them. But I have no clue what you're talking about with the proper arch or whatever." He didn't want to let go of her hand, but he did, taking his finger and running it across her eyebrow. "It looks perfect to me."

She swallowed, and her eyes met his, but maybe what he was feeling was showing too strongly in them, because she looked down before closing her eyes.

He ran his finger over the other eyebrow. Who even thought about eyebrows? He had no idea there was a proper shape for eyebrows.

"Everybody should have their eyebrows shaped just like this. Whatever shapes these are, they're my favorite. Along with these." He ran his fingers lightly over the freckles on her nose, and he allowed himself to smile, since her eyes were still closed, when she shivered.

He liked that.

That she was feeling what he was.

Using a single finger, he traced the knot in her nose, and her lips tilted up, her eyes still closed. "This is beautiful to me because I have a memory attached to it. Not everybody knows exactly what their wife looks like with a catheter bag lying across her face."

"You always were so romantic," she said without opening her eyes.

"Only with you." He heard the humor in his voice, and her eyes fluttered open. They weren't teenagers anymore, but if someone were to come in on them now, with their goofy grins, they'd be hard-pressed to believe they were adults in their thirties.

"That's true. I put too much store in other things and didn't appreciate that. Because it really was only me. Thank you." Her eyes drifted down as her smile faded. "I'm sorry I got upset about the things you didn't remember, instead of appreciating the things you did."

"Hey," he said, putting his finger under her chin, pushing up and over, trying to get her eyes to meet his. "I made just as many mistakes. More. I could spend the rest of tonight apologizing. Probably I should. Because a blanket 'I'm sorry' really isn't going to cut it any more than a blanket 'thank you.' If you don't know what you're apologizing for or thanking someone for, what's the point?"

"It's a start."

"It's not a good enough start."

"It is for me." Her brows, those brows that she insisted were hideous, lifted, like a challenge.

He grinned a little. "I don't agree with you when you say your brows are hideous. I think they're expressive. Right now, you're challenging me. And I know I'm right. You can't just say I'm sorry and expect to cover everything you've ever done wrong. And you can't just say thank you without explaining why you're saying it."

"Okay." She shrugged a little and smiled.

"Now I'm suspicious. Why are you agreeing so easily?"

She laughed. "It's a habit that I've tried to establish in the last eight years. Agreeing rather than arguing. I'm not very good at it, but I'm practicing right now."

He laughed. "You're trying to change your entire personality?"

It was her turn to laugh. "Is it that bad?"

He nodded. "I'm sorry, but yeah. If you agree with me, I start to think you probably hit your head, possibly broke your nose again, and I start thinking about emergency rooms and catheter bags."

"Well, since you think that stuff is cool, I'm glad I can help you think positively."

"It scares me."

"Good. I think that someone needs to keep you on your toes. I think you've gotten complacent now without me around to scare you once in a while."

His smile faded, and he snapped the flashlight off, leaning back against the wall, with his head pointed toward the ceiling.

"I don't like it when you scare me."

"Sorry. I didn't mean to go there."

She didn't have to say anything more for him to know she was thinking about her pregnancy and the birth of their twins as he was.

By far, the NICU had been the scariest place he'd ever been. The most stressful, the saddest, and yet somehow through it all, he'd grown closer to Emerson, closer to the Lord.

That didn't mean he hadn't been scared.

"You don't have to think about it. Everything's fine. It all turned out okay."

"I thought I was going to lose you. I thought I was gonna lose them. It's funny, how you only have to see your baby...not even see them, just know that they were growing inside of you, to love them fiercer than anything in this world except my wife. The idea of losing them rivaled the idea of losing you. I never want to go through that again."

"And I'm sure you won't. I don't think God makes us go through things like that twice. Although all in all, looking back, it was one of the best experiences of my life."

His head jerked around. "You can't mean that."

"I do. We entered that hospital a couple of scared kids. We came out parents in every sense. More mature. Closer to each other. And there was a new depth to our spiritual walk that hadn't been there when we'd walked in."

He had to agree. To a point.

"I was thinking that was the beginning of the end."

"That's because it was."

Neither one of them said anything for a few minutes, and he wished he was still holding her hand. It was somewhere in the darkness, but he wanted to be holding it.

Having Emerson beside him in the NICU was what had made that whole experience bearable. Even though now he looked back on it as a mostly good experience. At the time, it was the hardest thing he'd ever gone through.

He didn't know how long they sat like that in the darkness, each of them wrapped up in their own thoughts. Maybe this wasn't something they could work out, because he didn't know where to start.

But then her voice echoed in the stillness.

"I hadn't considered this until just now, when we were talking about how both of us thought that going through being in the NICU with our babies had been such a growing experience. You know, even that massive debt that we had, after we got out, that could've been a growing experience too. But I didn't handle it very well, and instead of letting it be a growing experience that moved us closer together, it was the thing that tore us part."

He sighed and hung his head. "You can't take all the blame for that. And I think you're right. Of course. I never saw it either. The NICU felt like the trial. But that was only one of them. We went through that beautifully. But we failed the second one, didn't we?"

"We did. Mostly my fault. You were the one who wanted to work it out."

"But the way that I wanted to work it out wasn't the way you wanted to. I could have compromised. I could have met you halfway."

"I never thought of that."

"Probably because I wouldn't entertain any thought of your dad's money. I wasn't going to take a penny from him. I was the man, and I would provide. But looking back, that was probably too scary for you."

"You're right. It was scary. I had two babies. I was overwhelmed. My dad would make everything go away, and you refused. He said he would pay every single cent of it, and he did."

"I know. I lost my wife and my pride." Maybe there was a little bit of drama in his voice, but that's how it felt at the time.

"I'm sorry." There was a long pause. "Maybe it's just taken me a few years to get a little older and a little wiser, but I can see now that a man's pride is a sensitive thing, and I didn't treat that any more sensitively than you treated my desire to have all the dates that were important to me remembered and celebrated."

He never compared it like that, but he supposed she was probably right. Although being prideful wasn't exactly something he was proud of. If that made sense. It probably didn't. He could see a million ways he could have done things differently. Now, when it was too late to go back and fix anything.

Chapter Sixteen

It was funny how sometimes the dark made her able to see things more clearly. One of those odd contradictions in life.

How giving rather than getting made a person happy.

Being kind to people who were unkind to you made you a better person.

Serving made one stronger, and surrendering your will was harder than demanding your own way.

All biblical principles she'd learned in childhood but never really understood.

The dark making one see things clearly wasn't exactly a biblical principle, but the light always shone brighter in the darkness.

Maybe that was the idea behind knowing what was right but not actually knowing what it was until the dark took away her sight and she could actually think about it.

She'd been in the dark plenty of times, but not with Reid in the last eight years.

The other things they'd argued about, remembering dates, her being bossy, and all those silly things that didn't matter. Maybe they had weakened their relationship enough that when the major trial came along, they were ready to go for the easy solution.

Or what had seemed like the easy solution. It was actually the harder one.

"I don't think I ever would have left if I'd realized that I was never coming back."

"Never?"

"Isn't that the saying, water under the bridge? You can never go back."

"Sometimes roads circle back. Rivers do too."

"Not to where they began."

"Maybe they turn into something better down the road." His voice sounded thoughtful, although there was a quality in it that she couldn't quite figure out, but it matched her mood too.

"Do you think?"

"I don't know. Maybe the river reference wasn't a good one. Maybe I ought to simply talk straight." He took a breath, like he was going to do exactly that and needed a little extra courage. "I think we made a stupid mistake. I think I was prideful and uncompromising. And I'm sorry. If it makes you feel any better, I don't know if there's been a day these past eight years when I haven't wished that I could go back and do it differently."

"Me too." Her words were whispered, words she never thought she'd say to him.

"It's probably true that we'll never have what we had. But I think it could also be true that we could have something better."

"That sounds so good I can hardly hope that it could be true."

"Let's make it be true."

"That simple?"

"Does it have to be complicated?"

"I guess not. But I need to apologize. I insisted that my dad needed to take care of things, and it showed a lack of trust in you. It hurt you. I didn't realize, not really, how badly I hurt you until just now, as I was thinking about it. We're kind of talking about how I looked, and you never doubted me, you never made me feel bad. If you said 'yeah, your nose is crooked, and I don't really like that,' maybe it wouldn't have been devastating, but it would've hurt. And yet, that's really what I did to you. I said I didn't trust you to take care of us, and I let my dad do it."

He was silent beside her, although she could feel his chest going up and down in the darkness. She leaned closer, and his arm brushed hers. It almost sounded like he was not quite panting, but there was no doubt her words had affected him.

"I would never have told you that," he said, his words barely a whisper. "That's not something I could admit to just anyone."

"I know it's probably hard to admit it to me, because once somebody hurts you, it's so hard to trust them again. I never did anything unkind, I was never mean, I never physically hit you, but my lack of belief in you destroyed what we had spent so many years building. It's just obvious to me now, when I was so blind before. I don't even know why I couldn't see that. Maybe I was just so caught up in being right—"

"Because you were right. What you wanted was the best thing to do. It would have been stupid to do anything else. And we've always agreed that you were the best one with money. Anytime we've done what you suggested, we've been good. It's not that I can't do anything, you just have a better grasp on finances than I do."

"I don't know about that—"

"I do. I might as well tell you now. The farm's in trouble. I borrowed a bunch of money and built a big dairy barn. Those are the buildings that you mentioned when you first came. But the price of milk tanked, and I lost my contract before I ever put a cow in her."

"Oh my goodness." Dread pulled in her stomach. And compassion. And disbelief, that he would even say that to her after the way she'd treated him. That he would admit something so hard.

"How much?" she asked gently, unsure if he'd trust her with that much.

"A half a million."

"What are you going to do?"

He shifted. "I don't know. I probably won't have much of a choice. I've got a good crop of corn, and I can pay all of my regular bills, but I can't even begin to touch that loan. I probably have until the beginning of the year, and then I'll lose the farm. I think I'll just let it go, start new somewhere else."

"You're kidding. You'll just let it go?"

His hand moved in the darkness, almost like he was lifting it up. "What else is there to do? I don't see any other solutions."

She didn't say anything and figured she better not. Maybe he'd let her look at the books, maybe she could figure something out, but not tonight.

"Would it hurt your feelings if I say I don't care?"

Even though it was dark, she could tell his head spun toward her, like he was searching out her face in the darkness.

"Thanks," he said with a heavy dose of sarcasm.

"Not like that. I mean that doesn't make any difference in what I've been saying, what I've said, the apologies I've made, and...how I feel."

"Oh. Don't you want to gloat a little? After all, this is the second time in the last decade that I've been in serious financial trouble."

"Maybe this is just God giving us a chance to do it again. And handle it the right way."

He snorted. "Really, He doesn't need to be that generous."

She laughed a little. "Seriously. This is almost the exact same thing that came between us before. And maybe you weren't getting it from what I'd said earlier, but what I was trying to say was that I regretted what I had done. Regretted it and wish I could change it."

"You're not involved in this. I mean, what are you gonna do? You can't leave me again when you're already gone."

She sat up, pulling her legs up and crossing them, and staring down, with her lips pursed, breathing in deeply like she was getting ready to jump off a cliff. Because that's what it felt like. Fear, anticipation, and that adrenaline high when you just throw yourself out there and have no idea what the result will be. It was all flowing together and swishing inside of her.

One more deep breath and she lifted her head, and looked at him, and said clearly, "Maybe I want to come back. What would you say to that? If I said I wish I'd never left, and I want to come back to Missouri, back to this farm, back to you. I never stopped being your wife, but I want to be your wife here, beside you."

Her hands trembled. She clenched them in her lap, and her breath shook. She closed her eyes and leaned her head back, pointing her face toward the ceiling, and waited.

And waited.

"What would I say? Is that what you wanted to know?" He paused. "This is a hypothetical question?"

She opened her mouth to answer, but his finger landed on her cheek and slid down to her lips.

"Forget that. I'll pretend it's real." A short pause that felt like forever. "Emmy. I want that. I want that more than anything. No. What I want more than anything is to be with you. I was thinking maybe it would be a good thing for me to lose the farm. Maybe I would start over again...in Switzerland. If that's where you are. Because wherever you are is where I want to be."

She still had trouble breathing, but for a completely different reason. "I take it back. I said earlier that you are not romantic. That's not true. This is the most romantic thing you've ever said to me."

"You better enjoy it. I'm not sure there's any more where that came from. I didn't mean to be romantic. I was just telling you the flat-out truth."

"Sometimes the truth takes courage."

"You're right about that." There was a small pause. "You ready for another truth? One that takes courage?"

"I think so. Is it going to be a hard one?" Her palms itched, and she tried to think of what in the world else he could say that would be worse than the things he'd already said.

"I want to kiss you. That's a hard truth."

Oh, boy. She opened her mouth so only the honest truth would come out. "Maybe a hard truth, but an easy answer. I want to kiss you too."

He grunted. "Then I have to wonder why we're still sitting here talking each other."

"Maybe we needed to talk before we can kiss again."

"I'll give you that...we haven't talked enough?"

She chuckled. "If I say no, will you keep talking to me?"

"If you say no, but promise that you'll eventually kiss me, yes. I'll keep talking. That's quite a reward to work for."

"Talking to me isn't supposed to be work."

"It's not. It's my second favorite thing."

She laughed. "I suppose your first favorite thing is kissing?"

"Maybe. Maybe it involves kissing." His hand touched her cheek before sliding down and settling on her neck as his thumb traced the line of her jaw.

"Hmm. That sounds interesting. Maybe we can talk about that a little." There was a small tremble in her voice.

"I think it's better if I show you." His fingers threaded through her hair. She leaned closer, putting her hand on his chest to keep her balance.

"Maybe I don't want to do the kissing thing. Maybe I want to keep touching like this. It feels a little different than it used to."

His lips moved, and she could hear him smile.

"I'm pretty sure we can work that in with the kissing. I think we were pretty talented that way."

"Oh? This takes talent?"

"Sure does. As I recall, you might have hideous eyebrows, but you had a heaping pile of talent."

"I can't believe you just called my eyebrows hideous."

He laughed. "You'd better be joking about that. Because you know for a fact I don't think your eyebrows are hideous." His laugh abruptly cut off, although his thumb continued to trace her jaw, and she didn't even bother trying to hide the fact that it made her shiver.

"If you think *your* eyebrows are hideous, are you perhaps harboring some resentment about *my* eyebrows?" He gave a dramatic pause. "Do you need to get some of your aggression toward my eyebrows out?"

"No. I'm jealous of your eyebrows. They're perfect. Unlike mine. Which are not arched—"

"In the proper way. They are arched on the outside, instead of on the inside? Is that right?" He laughed.

She was serious about her eyebrows. They were awful. But how could she be upset about them when he was so obviously uncaring? If he didn't give a flip about her eyebrows, she shouldn't either.

She barely had that thought when his head came down, and his lips landed on her eyebrow. Feather soft, and his breath brushed out, down her cheek, like a caress. His head lifted, and his lips touched her other eyebrow. "Perfect eyebrows. I love them."

Her eyes were closed, and she was savoring his touch, but she managed to say, "You've never even noticed my eyebrows. You just said that like ten minutes ago."

"Instalove," he murmured.

She smiled, her hand tracing down his ribs, harder and deeper than she remembered, which made her sad and curious at the same time. Sad that she missed the changes, and curious as to the other ones.

His lips brushed softly against her nose. "Love your nose. Always have. Even when it was straight."

She laughed again. "Seriously? Are you trying to make me laugh? Aren't we going to get serious and start kissing? I'm pretty sure you're not supposed to laugh while you're kissing."

"I think we've tried that before. Pretty sure teeth become a problem."

"That'll be just lovely. If you chip my teeth, and we have to pull boards off the shed so that we can go to the emergency dentist to get my teeth put back in..."

"You really think I'd pull boards off the shed? If I do that, someone just has to put them back on. Probably me. Can't you wait 'til morning?"

"How about you just stop making jokes, and that way we won't have to worry about my teeth chipping."

"I like the lady's assumption that my teeth are stronger than hers. Good one." His breath brushed over her lips. His voice came from right in front of her.

"I kind of think that was a challenge. Maybe we'll have to see whose teeth are stronger." She shook her head. "What am I saying? Normal people do not argue about whose teeth are stronger. What is wrong with you?"

"There's nothing wrong with me. Everything is right with the world. My wife is exactly where she belongs. And I think she might be staying. I'm sorry, that makes me happy. And not romantic."

"I don't think they're mutually exclusive. I think you can be happy and romantic and funny all at the same time, although I don't think we can have a teeth strength contest and still be happy and romantic."

"Noted."

She started to roll her eyes, but then his lips touched hers, and she lost every desire to move anything and could only think about his lips moving over hers and the pounding of her heart that matched the pounding of his under her hands. She slid them around shoulders that had broadened and filled out and pressed closer.

They weren't in the apple orchard all over again, and they weren't fifteen again either, but it felt like it, as everything was new and different and compelling and almost overwhelming.

She'd missed talking to him, she'd missed goofing with him, she'd missed his company and his presence and his comfort, but she'd also missed this, the passion that flared between them, the feeling that it was totally right, the right touch, the right scent, the right taste, the right feel. Even though he was so much different than she remembered, he felt perfect under her fingers and palms.

She pressed into him, and he fell back, taking her with him until she lay on top of him, her hair a curtain around them, and their lips and hands touching with an urgency that was probably natural and expected after being apart for eight years.

That urgency seemed to catch her up and pull her. There was no fear, no thought of going back, because being with Reid always felt right, and this was exactly where she wanted to be.

Chapter Seventeen

R eid lay spooned with his wife, his front at her back, his legs behind hers, and her feet, which had been cold at times during the night, pressed against the tops of his.

Was it possible that he even missed her cold feet?

He tucked his arm more tightly around her and pressed his nose and lips into her hair. Yes. He even missed her cold feet.

He just hoped he could keep from being an idiot again. He couldn't let his stupid pride dictate how he treated his wife. Or the direction his life went.

He wasn't so cocky and arrogant that he thought he'd fixed everything himself, just by saying he was sorry.

He figured he was probably due for a lot more humbling experiences before his life was over.

A lazy grin stole over his face. Humbling himself wasn't that bad. He'd woken up this morning holding his wife, and he'd had a pretty good night. Maybe apologizing had more benefits than what he had given it credit for.

"I can see your satisfied smirk," Emerson said sleepily.

Said satisfied smirk grew bigger. "Oh yeah?"

"Oh yeah. Now I can hear it, too." She moved against him, and he dropped his lips down to kiss the sensitive spot on her neck below her ear.

"Now you can feel it."

"I didn't quite catch that. Maybe you'd better do it again."

He chuckled and dropped another slower, lighter kiss in the same spot, just brushing his lips against her neck, and he was rewarded with a shiver.

"How much time do you think we have before the kids show up?" he asked, moving slightly lower and feathering a kiss on her sensitive skin again.

"Surely they're not going to show up at the break of dawn, are they?" she said, her words a little muffled, still sleepy, but laced with a seductive undertone that had everything to do with his lips on her neck.

"I doubt it," he said, his voice low in her ear. "I feel like that's a risk I'm comfortable taking."

He could hear the laughter in her voice when she said, "I don't know what that says about me, that I'm willing to take that exact same risk. It's kind of scary."

"I like it. The woman has gotten bolder." He laughed. "I think the tips of your ears are getting red. I wasn't really talking about last night, but I suppose that applies."

She twisted in his arms, pushing back, and he gave way, allowing her to turn, moving back until she lay on top of him, her hands on either side of his face, peering down. "I can show you bolder."

"Go right ahead. Do it before the kids get here."

———

Dallas walked along beside Houston, after getting out of Uncle Deacon's pickup, kicking the ground and wishing they hadn't done what they did.

He'd felt guilty all night for locking his parents in the shed.

Even though Uncle Deacon and even Grandma said it was okay, he'd never disrespected his parents like that.

Houston and he didn't exactly disobey, but he knew they hadn't been good kids.

He already had so much trouble sitting still, concentrating on his schoolwork, not talking when he was supposed to be listening, and giving both his dad and his mom such a hard time, without really meaning to, that he hadn't meant to make things worse for them.

Uncle Deacon walked along beside them, answering a question Houston had asked about what the Bible meant about harvesting in his life.

Dallas wasn't sure how Houston came up with those questions. He'd never even thought to question what kind of harvest a person had that wasn't done with equipment and didn't have an actual product to sell.

It made him feel like he wasn't as smart as Houston. Although Houston assured him that Dallas had things he was good at that Houston wasn't. Like driving. And running equipment. And sometimes he could talk their mom into doing stuff, while Houston said he never could. So maybe Dallas had what Grandma called the Hudson charm.

Grandma seemed to love him just fine, and so did his mom and dad.

Still, he felt kind of miserable because of what he'd done. His stomach knotted and twisted as they walked closer to the shed.

His parents knew that stuff like this was always his idea, and he would probably take the brunt of whatever anger they had.

"Do you think it worked?" he asked for about the thousandth time.

Uncle Deacon grinned and ruffled his hair. Uncle Deacon looked a lot like Dad, and his touch was just the same, a little rough, which Dallas liked, but he could tell when Uncle Deacon touched him that he really liked him.

"If that didn't work, I don't think anything will." Uncle Deacon's smile didn't dim, but Dallas noted that his eyes didn't smile with his mouth.

That made his stomach cramp even tighter.

As they approached the shed, Deacon said, "Okay, boys. You two stop here, and I'll knock on the door."

"Aren't you going to open it?" Houston asked.

"I think we'd better knock."

Houston looked over at Dallas, with his brows furrowed. Dallas shrugged. They had no idea why Uncle Deacon would knock on the door first.

"Maybe it has something to do with finding out how angry they are before he opens the door?" Dallas whispered.

Houston pursed his lips and nodded thoughtfully. "That's probably it," he whispered back.

They stood side by side as Deacon lifted his hand.

"What are you guys doing down there? Breakfast is up here on the table. Come on up and have yourself some. Bet you boys are hungry, unless Grandma fed you."

"Dad?" Houston said, as they all three turned and looked at their dad standing on the porch.

Dallas swallowed. "Where's Mom?" Surely Dad wouldn't have done anything to her.

Surely he wouldn't have escaped from the shed and somehow locked Mom in it? If that happened, they were both in really big trouble. Actually Dad was probably in really big trouble too.

But his fears eased when his mom stepped around from behind his dad and stood on the porch with him, her arm around him. Then, while Dallas watched, Dad's arm went around Mom, and he hugged her to him.

Dallas's mouth dropped, and he smiled at the same time. It was the exact same expression that Houston had on his face when Houston looked over at him.

It was funny, the way he could always tell what Houston was thinking. Even not having grown up with him, it didn't matter. He could see the celebration coming over his face, and he lifted his own hands up, slapping them with a double high-five and shouting and jumping and grabbing each other and hugging and jumping and yelling until they had jumped and tripped over each other and fallen down, and then they rolled on the ground, hugging each other and laughing and yelling.

Until they both, at the exact same moment, scrambled to their feet and went running to their parents, wrapping their arms around both of them. Dallas tried not to jump up and down while he was doing it, because he knew that annoyed people, but he was just so happy he could hardly stand still, so he jumped off the porch, running around the house, shouting and screaming, until he made it the entire way around and came back up on the porch where Houston was still hugging his parents, and he gave him another hug.

"It worked! It worked! I didn't think it was going to work. I thought we were going to be in big trouble. I thought Mom was going to be really mad, and then I thought Dad did something with Mom, but he didn't, and it all worked out because they like each other again —" He broke off abruptly. His eyes widened. "You're not going back to Switzerland, are you, Mom?"

Houston probably hadn't thought of it either, because his head jerked back. "This means you're staying here, right?"

One big boot landed on the porch. Uncle Deacon propped a leg on the porch and leaned an elbow on the top of his knee. "Hey, bro," Uncle Deacon said, like he was getting ready to ask about the weather.

Dallas wanted to squirm. He didn't want to talk about whether or not it was going to rain today or whether or not they were going to harvest corn. Although he was interested in that and did want to know, he had other things he wanted to know more, and he wasn't ready to have a casual conversation that Uncle Deacon seemed to be starting.

"Deacon. It appears I owe you."

Uncle Deacon didn't drop his gaze but looked steadily at Dad. Dallas had the feeling that Uncle Deacon found something funny.

"You can name him after me," Uncle Deacon said with a grin.

Dad pulled Mom tighter to him and squinted his eyes. "No way."

Houston looked over, and Dallas shrugged. He had no idea what they were naming. Did they get a puppy?

His eyes brightened at the thought. "I want to name it."

If they got a puppy, he wanted at least to have a say in the name. If Uncle Deacon named it, it would probably be named Moses or Hezekiah or something. That's what preachers did. Name things weird names.

"I think that's a good idea," Mom said.

Houston looked over him again, and they exchanged another shrug. From the way she was talking, they had been considering getting a puppy.

"That wasn't exactly what I was talking about anyway, bro," Dad said, looking at Uncle Deacon. "I actually meant I owe you a night locked in your woodshed. But I can try to make sure Blair's able to spend it with you."

Deacon grinned. "Don't forget I packed food, blankets, and a pillow. Plus I gave you a flashlight. I expect exactly the same kind of treatment. And you can lock Blair and me in the woodshed anytime you want to. As long as you keep Tinsley."

"Maybe all of our cousins can come over, we can have a big sleepover, cookout, campfire, and we can play in the creek and in the barn and make an obstacle course and have lots of food."

Houston nudged him with his shoulder, and Dallas snapped his mouth closed. He did have a tendency to say way more than he should. He knew he didn't stop talking the way other people did, but he couldn't figure out what was okay to say and when he needed to stop. Everything he said seemed important. He was interested in it anyway.

His dad looked down at him, with his arm still around Mom. "To answer your question, yes. Your mom is going to stay here, and both of you boys are too. We'll all live together, and we'll try hard to get along. All of us." Dad grinned the grin that Dallas always thought looked like a seesaw, with one side of his mouth up and one side down.

His mom looked up, and she seemed to like that grin too, because she reached up and touched his cheek right beside his mouth.

Then Dad leaned down and kissed Mom, right on the lips. Which, Dallas figured, was probably a good thing, but it was a little bit gross. And then they didn't stop kissing, and it got really gross, and this time when Houston looked at him, instead of exchanging shrugs, they exchanged horrified expressions. He'd seen kissing like that once or twice on TV, but he never thought anybody actually did it in real life. That was disgusting.

"I'd rather eat a worm," he muttered.

Behind him, Uncle Deacon laughed and then put a hand on each of their heads, ruffling their hair. "I think that's a really good idea. And I'm glad to hear it." His hands came off their heads, and he started to walk away. "Don't forget to remind your mom and dad about that puppy you guys are getting, as soon as they're done being disgusting. I'm heading home. Your dad's given me some ideas on some new techniques I can use with my wife in case we want to be disgusting."

———

"Is that the dog whining?" Emerson asked.

The hand on his chest making slow, light circles had stilled, and Reid wanted to take her hand and make her start again.

It'd been a week since the kids had locked them in the shed, and he supposed he should have punished them more than he had, but really, he wanted to thank them and be grateful. So that's what he'd done. He was a little sad that their ten-year-old twins were smarter than they were.

He supposed that was why his wife was now asking him if their puppy was whining at, he turned his head to look at the clock, 2:15 in the morning.

"I don't hear anything," he said, hoping she'd start with the circle motions on his chest again.

But her head lifted off his shoulder. "Really? You don't hear that? It sure sounds like the puppy? Like he's whining. It sounds sad."

"It's just your ear ringing. I'm pretty sure I can kiss you and make it go away."

"Reid. I'm serious. Can't you hear that?"

He turned his head and brushed his lips across the corner of her mouth. "I can. But the puppy's upset because he's not with his mom anymore, and there's nothing we're going to do about it, because neither you nor I look like her, smell like her, or have what she has that makes puppies happy. However," he said, brushing his lips against the corner of her mouth again, "you have something that makes me very happy, so at least, between the puppy and I, one of us can be happy."

"Seriously, Reid? You're just going to let the puppy whine?"

"How about we give him thirty minutes. If he doesn't stop at that point, we'll figure something out. And in order to stay awake for the next thirty minutes, do you have any ideas of what we could do?"

Her fingers started the circular motions on his chest again. "Hmm. Let me think...we could play a game of Parcheesi. That usually takes about thirty minutes, doesn't it?"

"Try again."

"You can give me a backrub. I can handle that for thirty minutes."

"Now she's getting warmer. I think I can rub the lady's back for five minutes." Definitely. "But I still have twenty-five minutes left. What next?"

Her finger made a big circle and then stopped, and her head lifted up. "You could think about the solution I have to your problem."

His breath caught. They hadn't talked about the farm, or the money, or her dad, or her job. Nor of them expecting her back before the end of the month. None of it, other than she was staying in Missouri. That's all he cared about.

He supposed there was a reason he was avoiding talking about that. He definitely didn't want to.

He started to move, tugging his arm, trying to take it out from underneath her head. "Never mind. I think I'll go get the puppy. It's whining."

"Reid, stop it." There was humor in her voice, but there was also a note that said that he'd better not walk away from this conversation.

He already knew it.

He bent the arm that was under her head until his fingers touched her hair, and he stroked back gently, reminding himself that having a relationship with his wife was more important than any pride or dumb ideas he had. They could talk about this, and he would definitely take whatever she said into consideration.

"You're right. We probably should talk about it. What's your idea?" He'd just been kind of figuring the bank would take the farm, and they could do something else. "You're not allowed to sell any kidneys. Not mine, not yours. We're not selling any kids' kidneys either. Although, we could possibly sell the dog's kidneys."

"You're not even funny. How do you come up with this stuff? We're not selling kidneys. Or livers or hearts or lungs or anything else that people actually need to survive."

"You only need one. You have two. God gave you a spare so you can share."

"I love it when you rhyme. You know that. But you're not distracting me. I have a solution, and I want to talk to about it."

Thunder rumbled in the distance, and Reid thought it was kind of appropriate as a background noise for this conversation. He almost mentioned it, but then he thought that maybe Emerson wouldn't find his humor as funny as she found his rhyming. Especially not after he suggested trying to sell her kidney to save the farm. Or was it her selling his? Wasn't sure, since he was a little distracted because her finger was still doing the circular motion thing but not on his chest anymore.

"Listening." That was mostly true.

"I talked to my dad. I told him I want to sell my share of the business. And I talked to the man that I've been working with for the past eight years, who wants to be a part of the business—he's willing to buy. He'll need a little bit of time to come up with the money, but it should be a smooth acquisition that would go through before Christmas. Which should be good enough to save the farm by New Year's. What do you think?"

Reid stared at the ceiling, wishing he'd just gone and gotten the dog the first time she said something.

Then he wouldn't be having this argument with himself.

He'd thought he'd conquered the pride thing, but he found he hadn't, because "no" was the word that sprang to his lips immediately. He bit it back before it came out.

There was a flash of light and more thunder. It sounded closer.

The whining got louder and more desperate.

Reid almost ended the conversation by saying he would go get the puppy. Instead, he rolled over onto his side, shifting his arm and laying his head on his shoulder, kind of propping it up. Emerson's legs tangled with his, and it made him smile at the contrast in texture and size. But he didn't get distracted.

"What you're saying is you want to use the money from the sale of your share of the business to pay off the loan that I got for the farm to build the dairy barn that didn't pan out?"

It didn't sound any better now as he said it out loud. Actually, it sounded worse. Everything in him rebelled. He'd been brought up to be the protector and provider, and he wanted to think of himself that way.

"I know you don't like the idea." She rolled toward him, her hand going to the indent of his waist. Her fingers moving. "I'm fine if we don't. I'm still selling my share, and the money is going in our joint account. I consider it ours. Just like I consider the farm ours, even though you've been the one paying on it since we got married. I don't look at things as mine and yours. We got married, two became one. Everything that I have is yours. If you want to make separations out of our stuff and split hairs, I don't care. But I'm not."

She didn't sound angry nor upset. She actually sounded kind of reasonable. Which of course was the way Emerson usually sounded.

"When you put it that way, it makes me look like an idiot if we don't do that."

"Your words," she said, a little flippantly, and he grinned.

"You are not going to twist my words to make me say that I just said I was an idiot. Not happening."

Her shoulder went up, and her fingernails scratched up his back, lightly, making goosebumps break out on his arms, and he shuddered.

A flash of light lit up the bedroom, blinking for a good three or four seconds, followed almost immediately by a loud and continuous crack of thunder.

The desperate whines became howls along with scratching. A door closed.

"Let's do that then. You sell your share of the business, and if you're sure that's okay, we'll pay off the loan for the farm and figure something else out. I've heard the price of eggs is up."

"I'll look into it," she said, a smile in her tone.

"Oh really?" he said. "Just like that?"

He twisted and rolled until she was on her back and he leaned over top of her. He was just lowering his head when the door burst open. Another flash of light, happening almost simultaneously with the deafening roar of thunder, and two little boys carrying a puppy crashed into the room and jumped on their bed.

He lowered his head to whisper in her ear as he rolled to his side, "I don't want you going back to Switzerland, but maybe the boys would like to visit their grandfather once in a while."

Epilogue

ndrew Coleman walked through the door of the feed store in Cowboy Crossing, his new canine companion, adopted from the shelter in nearby Trumball, following.

"I hope that's a meat tray. No one else has brought anything," Preston, one of the regular single dads who never missed a meeting, said.

"I told them to load it up," Andrew said, tilting the tray a bit to show Preston, who raised his brows – there really was a lot of meat on it – and grinned in anticipation.

From his own experience as a single dad, he knew exactly what that look meant – thank goodness someone else was providing supper. Cooking one's own got old.

"Hey, what's that?" Preston asked, looking at Andrew's dog as he held his hand out for the meat tray.

Andrew held the meat tray up, knowing that if he took his eye off it for a second, his new companion would not hesitate to snatch it out of his hand and devour it, plastic parts and all.

"Looks like a cross between a German Shephard, a Husky and a jack rabbit," Ransom said with a smirk. He, too, eyed the meat tray.

Andrew should have brought two. Meat trays, not dogs. The one dog he'd gotten had been way more than he had been bargaining for. And he'd only had her six hours.

"Does she have a name?" Preston asked, taking the lid off the meat tray with one hand and holding it with his teeth while he pulled about four rolled slices off the artfully arranged masterpiece and managed to shove them in his mouth while pulling the lid out, all with one hand.

Andrew might have taken exception to the lid being in his friend's mouth, except, even if no one else showed up for the single dad's meeting, there was no chance there would be any left overs.

"Gladys," Andrew said, wishing he'd thought of a new name before he'd brought her. That's the name she'd come with. He hated it, but hadn't come up with anything better. He'd been too busy cleaning up the couch that she'd managed to destroy while he'd walked out to chat with the mailman and give him letters and money for stamps.

While he'd been cleaning up the couch, Gladys had managed to chew off the end of the most expensive pair of skis he owned, and while he was still lamenting the loss of the skis, she'd escaped from the brand new cage he'd bought before he'd gone to pick her up and chewed the nylon rope that he'd only used once – when he'd climbed Mt. Rainier four summers ago.

It had been his last mountain, but old dreams died hard and he'd been hanging onto his equipment and had done some less challenging climbs in the Ozarks. No rope work.

As he'd been expecting, his buddies burst into laughter.

"Gladys?" Ransom said, still chuckling. "Who names anything Gladys?"

Maybe that hadn't been her original name. Maybe her previous owner had wanted to saddle her with a name that befitted her hideous personality.

Andrew tightened his lips, guilty.

From her perspective he'd brought her home to a completely new environment and then basically abandoned her for the mail lady.

Ransom reached out to pet Glady's head. A growl rumbled in her throat just before her teeth snapped. Thankfully, Ransom had quick reflexes and her jaw closed on nothing but air.

Oh, great. She destroyed his house and now she was going to bite his friends.

"Testy," Ransom muttered.

"Looks like she'll be a great watch dog," Preston said, taking a step back and adjusting his stance into more of a protective one – protecting the meat tray.

That was the first time Gladys had shown any aggression at all. Andrew wasn't sure if he should be worried or not.

A wet nose shoved into his palm.

She was so affectionate. Almost needy. He appreciated the affection, needed it, really. Since there wasn't anyone else in his life caring about him.

But, he was still harboring a grudge about his skis. The couch... not so much. He'd just shoved the foam back into the cushions and flipped them upside down so the rips didn't show. It was still usable. Still had a lot of life left in it.

He turned his hand and scratched her ears. They were kind of big. She had the elegant face of a German Shephard, but ears only a mother would love.

And him. Andrew supposed he could grow to love her ears. If she didn't chew any more of his skis. Or bite his friends.

"It's not Christmas yet, man."

Andrew turned. Reid and Deacon Hudson had just walked in together. He shook their hands.

"Six weeks left. Figured there wasn't any chance of winning, so I decided I'd capitulate and adopt."

"Weren't you supposed to get two?" Preston asked, chugging a drink before shoving more meat into his mouth.

"No way." Holy smokes, he wasn't even sure he was going to be able to handle this one dog. Gladys. No way was he getting two. "That was you. Two cats."

"I haven't given up yet," Preston said, his mouth full. "Some chick's gonna meet me and beg me to marry her." He swallowed. "I haven't decided if I'm gonna say yes yet. Think I'll ask to taste her sticky rolls first."

"Pretty sure that's sexist and will probably get you thrown in prison. That's after she slaps your face good," John said. He'd walked in after Reid and Deacon and already had both hands in the meat tray, which was more than half gone. Guess they were going low carb tonight.

They all laughed. John had been joking and they knew it. He was just acting arrogant and cocky to hide the fact that he didn't have any prospects, none at all, and was probably going to lose the bet, too.

"Really, Andrew, you shouldn't give up. There's six weeks until Christmas. A lot can happen between now and then." Deacon shoved a hand in his pocket, his stance casual, but his eyes sincere, even probing.

Andrew looked down at Gladys, with her sweet brown eyes that looked up at him adoringly. One would never guess she'd destroyed over a thousand dollars' worth of stuff in less than four hours.

He didn't want to disagree with Deacon. He also knew Deacon had been rumored to be a bit of a match maker.

Andrew hadn't believed the rumors at first, but slowly each of Deacon's brothers had gotten remarried, and there definitely were some interesting circumstances going on. An auction. A celebrity chef just showing up in Cowboy Crossing. Rumors of a couple being stuck in a bathroom, of all places, and another couple locked in a shed overnight. Scary stuff.

Andrew had vowed to keep his distance from Deacon. Adopting the dog had been one way to put some distance between himself and Cowboy Crossing's preacher, who was apparently scrounging extra income by playing Cupid. As far as Andrew knew, Deacon had officiated at every ceremony – except his own – and he was probably making a pretty penny with all the weddings in town. The "bet" that Andrew would be married by Christmas was probably made in hopes that Deacon would have a little extra spending money around the holidays.

Andrew patted Gladys's head and looked back up at Deacon. The other men had moved off, and Andrew glanced over at them.

His thoughts were uncharitable. If there was any matchmaking going on, Deacon only wanted the best, and, honestly, Reid looked about as happy as a man could look, which is the way the rest of Deacon's brothers seemed nowadays.

Deacon wasn't doing a bad thing.

"I think I'm happy with Gladys," he finally said. Maybe they were happier with wives and companions. But Andrew already had an ex who lived two thousand miles away with his boys that he seldom got to see. Odds were good that if he'd screwed up once, he'd do it again.

He'd just be happy with Gladys. Although if she destroyed his house and bit his friends, she might end up being as big of a mistake as his ex.

————

Join Jessie's list and be the first to know about new releases and sales on her books!

Read My Dearest Reagan, originally titled *A Mistletoe Mishap in the Show Me State*, the next book in the Cowboy Crossing series. A man who hides fear with courage. A woman who needs a house but longs for a home. And the dog with anxiety issues who brings them together. Keep reading for a sneak peek now.

A Gift from Jessie

View this code through your smart phone camera to be taken to a page where you can download a FREE ebook when you sign up to get updates from Jessie Gussman! Find out why people say, "Jessie's is the only newsletter I open and read" and "You make my day brighter. Love, love, love reading your newsletters. I don't know where you find time to write books. You are so busy living life. A true blessing." and "I know from now on that I can't be drinking my morning coffee while reading your newsletter – I laughed so hard I sprayed it out all over the table!"

Claim your free book from Jessie!

Escape to more faith-filled romance series by Jessie Gussman!

The Complete Sweet Water, North Dakota Reading Order:

Series One: Sweet Water Ranch Western Cowboy Romance (11 book series)

Series Two: Coming Home to North Dakota (12 book series)

Series Three: Flyboys of Sweet Briar Ranch in North Dakota (13 book series)

Series Four: Sweet View Ranch Western Cowboy Romance (10 book series)

Spinoffs and More! Additional Series You'll Love:

Jessie's First Series: Sweet Haven Farm (4 book series)

Small-Town Romance: The Baxter Boys (5 book series)

Bad-Boy Sweet Romance: Richmond Rebels Sweet Romance (3 book series)

Sweet Water Spinoff: Cowboy Crossing (9 book series)

Small Town Romantic Comedy: Good Grief, Idaho (5 book series)

True Stories from Jessie's Farm: Stories from Jessie Gussman's Newsletter (3 book series)

Reader-Favorite! Sweet Beach Romance: Blueberry Beach (8 book series)

Blueberry Beach Spinoff: Strawberry Sands (10 book series)

From Strawberry Sands to: Raspberry Ridge (12 book series)

Swoonfully Jolly Holiday Stories:

Holiday Romance: Cowboy Mountain Christmas (6 book series)

Cowboy Mountain Christmas Spinoff: A Heartland Cowboy Christmas (9 book series)

New and Much Loved: Mistletoe Meadows (4 books and counting!)

Laughing Through the Snow: Christmas Tree, PA Sweet Romcoms (6 short reads)

They were high school sweethearts, but money and pride came between them. Can their twin sons trick them into falling in love again?

Reid Hudson would be happy on his Missouri farm except he'd always thought he'd be sharing it with his soulmate, Emerson. Instead, he gets six months with each of his boys and splits the holidays. Not the life he'd planned.

Emerson Mahoney hadn't expected her family to fall into a fortune. When her new husband flatly refused to use any of their money to ease the financial burden from the birth of their twins, she couldn't believe how hard-headed he was. She'd taken the opportunity to fly to the Swiss Alps and become a temporary member of her father's new business team, never expecting it to last eight years.

When one of their boys deliberately misses his flight to stay on the farm with his twin brother in Missouri, Emerson is forced to come back to the states and confront the husband she is still married to and the man she'd never fallen out of love with.
When fuel shortages ground all airplanes, she's forced to spend a month on the farm.

Can their twins trick them into falling in love again?

USA Today best-selling author Jessie Gussman writes sweet and inspirational romance from her farm in central Virginia. Having attended, but never graduating from the school of hard knocks, Jessie uses real life on the farm to inspire her cowboy, rural and blue-collar fiction.

ISBN 979-8-89382-094-2

They Never Wanted Me to Wake Up to My Anointing

Yvette Roland